The Shingle Maker

And Other Tales

Also by Hermann Stehr from K A Nitz:

The Engraver

Meicke, the Devil

The Shingle Maker

And Other Tales

Hermann Stehr

K A Nitz
LOWER HUTT

Der Schindelmacher, *Gerichtet* and *Der Besuch*
all published in the
Gesammelte Werke edition of
Auf Leben und Tod 1927

These translations by Kerry Nitz
Copyright © K A Nitz 2012
All rights reserved

ISBN: 978-0-473-21589-7

National Library of New Zealand Cataloguing-
in-Publication Data

Stehr, Hermann, 1864-1940.
The shingle maker and other tales / by
Hermann Stehr ; translated
by Kerry Nitz.
ISBN 978-0-473-21589-7 (pbk.)—ISBN 978-
0-473-21590-3 (online)
I. Nitz, Kerry, 1971- II. Title.
833.912—dc 23

Contents

The Shingle Maker

The wooden gutter stuck out so far from the shingle roof that only a narrow, red strip of light was thrown on the barn floor by the sinking spring sun. It met the ground in about the middle of the space and disappeared for a moment into the curly, white wood shavings as old Franz Tone's whittle threw them down squeaking. Then the red light carved itself out of the clutter, jiggled trembling over the shavings and crept wearily up the barn wall, over the leather trousers of the farmer who was leaning there, broad and idle. That was probably the hardest on the weak evening light, as the farmer's trousers had been worked to a mirror-like sheen, and it found no rest. The few folds across them did not help it much either, for when it had lain down somewhere and grabbed a breath to move a little higher, the farmer had moved with his leg to the side each time, so that the poor light fell back again onto the barn wall. But what such a ray of light plans to do, it carries out whether it is alright with a farmer or not, especially when spring is sending it. So the strip of light in the barn did not slacken either in moving up the farmer's leg, on the straight path to the blank uniform's button on which one side of the yellow-clasped bib hung. And finally the farmer forgot himself because the shingle maker's whittle had come to a large branch. Then the ray of light moved further up entirely undisturbed and soon sat on the middle of the blank button, balanced back and forth on it, looked around cheerfully for a while, so that it sparkled in the dim space, and then skipped hastily with long strides out towards the sun ... trembling. It was freezing and the sun was blowing its last smouldering clouds into the black peaks of the nearby mountains.

Then it was evening and, deep in the forest, a scornful jay was still laughing alone.

"How quick the evening goes", the farmer said.

"Well yes, it's always like that in spring. Quickly dark, quickly light. Rolls like a child, pools and flickers in a little sack", the old man replied while he cut around a branch groaning.

"Rubbish!" the farmer flared up unburdening himself.

"Whoops, it's through", Franz Tone continued, letting go of the whittle with his right hand and wiping his narrow forehead with its bulging wrinkles. With that he shoved the large-brimmed cap back so that a large tuft of ice-grey hair welled out on each side of his head.

"It's hard sometimes, isn't it", the farmer took up the conversation over work again.

"When a branch is like this, then yes."

The shingle maker had opened his big mouth with its long, yellow teeth, and after he had finished the answer on which it waited, he emitted a rough groan, long and leisurely.

"How long have you been making shingles, Franz Tone?"

"Exactly ... in June it was ... forty ... forty-five years."

"A good few years."

"Yes, you were still a boy then ... if I may say so", the old man added respectfully.

"And what are you now?"

"How old?"

"Yes."

"Seventy-eight on the 17th of June."

"That's only eight days from now. You have a birthday on the Wednesday!?"

"Well — yes — yes — —"

The answer came hesitantly, forced, and, at the same time, Franz threw the whittle to the ground.

"But I won't see it either if the head goes into the grave a little."

"I believe it, Kroner ... but I know you."

"Well, that too.

That is, I feel it," the old man added with a seriousness that did not fit at all with his everyday words.

"Doesn't anything suit you?"

"Suit — oh now! — — who's asking me about it?" Then the shingle maker threw himself into the shavings, shoved both hands behind his head and stretched out his legs.

"Whoever lies in a coffin and can't be woken anymore, he has it good", he then said slowly and, at the same time, his eyes looked up fixedly at the brown roof trusses.

"You mean ... to ..."

Franz Tone just nodded quietly.

"Such thoughts would drive me away with a whip."

"Yes — — but to where!"

"Where they're from."

"But what if they come from within you?"

"Ah, no horse bites itself."

The shingle maker gave no answer. He just looked at Kroner from the side smiling bitterly.

Then, after a while, his big, black eyes glowed from under his heavy brows. The next moment, however, the old, rigid weariness again lay over his wide, roughly creased face with its grey stubble.

"It wouldn't be right with you — with you, haha, with you — and I don't know how it could be", he laughed, mocking himself, and spat as he turned his head to the side.

"Not with me, you're right, man," Kroner exclaimed in growing agitation and leapt up from his place of rest, "not with me, I'll also have to keep myself and get a place to retire to for a time like you. As long as I can guide a plough, I'll never throw up my hands. — — Hey, right isn't it, I still stick bread in my own mouth alone now when I'm hungry, and as much as I want. By the same token, the tame have to go and eat from a strange hand like a dog."

"You're right! — right — right — right ..."

With that the old man had sprung up hastily as though the farmer was digging a deep wound into his body with a sharp knife.

He slapped himself heavily on the chest and screamed out the first "right" agonizingly. Then his voice became softer and softer, and he looked helplessly in front of his feet after he had fallen completely silent.

"... right, all of it, all of it," he took the discussion up again, "straight from the heart, what you say. — — — But, my good man, when the near horse is missing from the two-in-hand, ha, when you get a slapping, then your courage will probably go like the midday mist, then it'll go — — — ha, and how else could it be?" —

"Now, Tone, you're kidding me again."

"How's that? ..."

The farmer fell silent and looked at him in astonishment.

But Franz was suddenly stimulated as though he had been drinking strong schnaps. He grasped a shingle and broke it in half with his bare hands.

"Well, and you say you're weak!" Kroner replied in unabashed wonder to the questioning look of the old man.

"Like a flatterer", was the dull answer. "Look, I'm battering a piece of gravel to powder with my hand, but love, love — ha, love!! — when I lost love, I knew what it was — —"

"Tone, dammit, Tone, you'll go mad or already are. You're flailing around like mad in front of me and have lost love? — Tone! — Tone!"

"Lost! — — it is nothing other than that, I can't help myself. It was that morning. — — —

The sun seemed to be screaming in my room when I awoke. — All was silent in the house. The miller was already clattering away.

Ha, Tone, I think to myself, are you deceiving yourself? A bright, clear day and the wife, the woman, is still sleeping? —

I turn around and look at her. She is sleeping like a stone. It must have been a bad night for her, I think, she is far too pale.

Then the cows are mooing in the barn, one trying to better the other. They are crying with hunger.

Now she'll spring up like the devil! And I was already pleasing myself with the big eyes she would make when she saw that they had been shut up and that I was already releasing them. — For I had quickly gotten out of bed and was standing, having just pulled my trousers on, and I turned to her and held my breath: — — — now! — — — now! — — — now! — The cows grumbled on.

She never stirred.

At once I began to shudder and it was like thousands of ants ran into my heart, so that it stopped for a moment, not knowing if it would continue beating or explode ...

And it occurred to me like a tied up clod, like a dumb cluck.

My wife!

I couldn't do anything else, I had to cry out.

And how that sounded: like when someone screams for help from far away, high, trembling, so weak.

But as the word came out, my fear grew into a mountain and I knew everything and was dying.

In my breast, however, it became fervent and slowly rose, the innermost slowly rose, from deep in my soul.

It got stuck in my throat. I wanted to swallow and tried to, but it didn't go forwards, nor back.

All of a sudden it didn't matter to me.

My wife!

I grasped her forehead ... a stone in the night. — — —

I walked out stiffly.

Outside I opened my mouth, then the hot beast in my throat caught my breath and travelled fervently from my mouth into the air.

See, farmer, that was my love. — —

My heart found itself again, but empty. My thoughts, but cold.

The drive belt was broken in two, the where and where-from that I'd never known brought sense into the swinging machine that a human body is.

I ploughed. I sowed. I hoed. I raised corn. And it was to me as though I never did anything, no, it was someone else, it was all the same to me.

It was to me, rather, like a bush when no breeze touches it — — dark, deadened.

Now, with the passing of the years, it's the seventh, it's already probably a little different. I can feel my unhappiness, more and more, hence when I was sowing a while ago, I felt my age. But I sowed, from edge to edge, so that I didn't feel too good ..." He broke off and stood silently as though frozen.

"Good night, farmer!"

He violently tore his eyes from the abyss in which they appeared to be looking and, in parting, stretched out his trembling hand to Kroner.

"Good night, Tone!" Kroner grasped the hand and held it. "But you have a child!"

"Seffie? — so you say!"

He said it as though his tongue was numb with pain. But when he saw that Kroner was listening quite taken aback, he added with anxious haste, "Child, yes, yes. My wife's sister's little girl, Ullrich's Seffie, a good child, good, good, the man too, Ullrich the husband, well then, then."

It was meant to sound convincing, but the bitterness screamed from the soft words which the poor man was saying with trembling lips.

"Don't you get enough to eat?" Kroner tore him from his brooding.

"Farmer, I actually get more than enough."

"But not a warm room?"

"She has a big oven in *her* room."

"Not easy?"

"She still spurs me on if I'm not working quick enough ... has nobody heard that yet?!"

Shocked at the words which he had spoken against his will, he looked around. Then he wished him, "Good night, once more."

The farmer silently offered him his hand.

Before he could find the words, the shingle maker had disappeared through the door. Slowly, thoughtfully, Kroner followed him.

"Tone!" he then called suddenly, making a decision. With the same anxious haste which had been noticed in his farewells, the shingle maker turned around as he was going, "I must go, otherwise I'll be late home." With that he hastened onwards.

"Yes, is it so?" — pondered Kroner — "oh, you dog! The business for nothing and now doing a good deed! — Just so! — No, Kroner, the washer of my corpse can take the handle from my hand, and nobody else.

Yes, I believe it all, poor, old Tone."

With that he went into the house.

When I go to heaven, it'll probably be so: you always go past the lights. But everything will change that now looks just like a glowworm, it will", the old man thought to himself while he climbed the Eschberg through the evening darkness to his home.

The light strip of the path wound in sharp turns through the grey shadowy expanses of the meadows on both sides. Flat stones, looking like bread in the uncertain light, were laid strewn here and there in the path.

Franz sought them with his feet, but it was not at all boggy.

Then he paused and counted the lights which were to be seen on the righthand side of the path at almost equal distances right up to near the peak of the mountain. The little houses from which they glowed were like formless haystacks.

"One, two, three ... eight; the stars start behind them. Who knows if that light is the light of men or a star? — Who knows? — —

Wasn't at all easy and good for me, old left behind, I'm walking on the row of lights now, raising my legs more and more, the higher I get

— nevertheless, if I feel a void under me, I'll just make a long stride. And as I do it, I'll avert my eyes. I have to push open somewhere. At one time, I'd give a jolt like a wagon that was stopping before an inn — mph! — then I'd go! — — — I'd look at the star — and the other stars twinkling around them, cosy like neighbours, the sparkling ones, the yellow ones, the red ones, and numbering to eternity. Hey! can I call for good luck a little lightman, you, where my one, my wife, probably lives: Katharina Umlauf, from Sauerborne, if you only know how to speak proper in heaven.

Ha, you see, old Tone, there, you were hard to please and a call comes from a distant twinkling light — mph! — cock the ears! — You recognise it from before: like the blue tit whistles, nice and long like an old maid — it knows the way straight to me. I know who is calling and making long legs in the blue near you, wife — a step, one all alone, and it would happen. Why, in all the world, why don't I make it then? Waiting does nothing for me!"

With an amorphous murmur, he conversed with his longing dream-thoughts. They came driving over him. He was climbing with powerful strides. He was breaking out in sweat. His stick was swinging heavily. His eyes gazed blankly, but only into that distance which was attached to the expanses of his inner being.

People walked past him. He did not see them.

"Something has come over Franz Tone", they said, watching after him and thinking, 'Who's seen the like?'

But the retiree did not notice anything and ran as though today he really wanted to enter the next world. The climb was already becoming leisurely. The two fields began to broaden into flats on the other side of which the mountain, with its last strength, was pushing up its peak from the shelter of the forest into the blue.

The humid night was talking to him, murmuring with the tree tops of the forest, water was burbling sleepily in the forest, and a lonely silhouetted spruce was moving its hanging branches in dream uniformly and silently over the peaked gable of a small house below it. It was the last human dwelling on the mountain and cowered like a black cat, nestled by the trunk of the tree. Lurking, the little house looked with the erratic light of its two window-eyes at the solitary wayfarer who was heading for it.

Franz Tone still believed he was climbing, or did he really want to take "the last step" now? Enough, he hastened raptly towards it with exceptionally high swings of his legs.

He neither heard the creaking of the door of the lonely house under the spruce nor did he see the prying woman stepping onto the path.

Ever murmuring, he ran straight into her.

Her arms propped on her hips indignantly, she stepped to the side, obviously to get confirmation that the old man was staggering home "drunk". Truly!

Then she could not master her fury anymore, "You, wanderer," she shrieked with a loathsome voice, "have you bucked yourself up? Pig! And how drunk you are. Shame on you now!"

She gave the shingle maker a shove. He paused and looked around doubting, "Yes, is that the sky? Well yes, yes! It must be true. I can already hear the angel singing."

"What angel? Now march in! Grey-headed ghost, do you think I'll stay open for you until fifteen?" —

Ripped from the heights of his wistful dreams, the shingle maker found himself on the sandbank of his lonely misery again.

It made the old man with his powerful figure, hard face and large, thoughtful eyes daunted and timid.

Uncertainly, he went straight to the furious woman, "Seffie, look, an old man simply pleases and provides for himself", he gently pleaded.

"An old ape, speaks too", her rash crudeness burst out. Then she laughed over her thought.

Meanwhile, her husband, lured from the house by her wild clamour, had also stepped over to them with firm, cautious strides. For a while he looked from one to the other.

"Hehe! — in such darkness and so loud? — Why's that? — why? What's it about? — Yes — That's our man!"

Franz backed away a step when he heard the softly quivering tone of the short, skinny man's ironic words.

"Don't fall, old man, it would be to much for me if you did yourself some harm", remarked the midget as he saw the retiree backing away.

Then he turned to his wife,

"Come, Seffie, don't get excited, it could do him harm in his state. — Good night, Tone, we've eaten already."

The old man followed the pair without a word of reply. The door had been thrown shut booming behind him. With hesitant, groping steps, he toddled to the door of his little room.

Truly, he was like a hollow eggshell and his vigour was nothing but a rough, useless husk. In the narrow room, which was more like the interior of a large crate with grated spy holes, he bumped against the ceiling because he had forgotten in his forlorn state to stoop.

"I'm pushed around everywhere. So I'll only have peace when I'm stretched out. —

Why don't I do it? — Why — why, I ask — why?" he asked himself, half voicing it, while he groped around in his room in futile restlessness.

"Here's the bed, like a dog's bed — the blankets are stiff with dirt and they stink — my shirts are like muck — I feel it, tempers, stinginess, no love, no laughter, no friendly face — everything in rags, my days, my senses, my work.

And who can fix it? — There's no tailor for it like death."

Suddenly he came to and was startled, as he was stooped over in the darkness before the windowless back wall and talking to the roof beams.

"Tone, that won't lead to a good end," he said to himself dully, "Kroner said so as well, said as well, as well" ... and the rest died in a shiver, as the consequences of his exhaustion now showed themselves.

He turned to the table by whose long side the bed stood and deposited on it the rest of his bread wrapped in a colourful handkerchief. He untied it with shivering hands in order to eat the hard, dry crusts for supper.

Unrelenting fatigue suddenly overcame him.

He shoved the bread away, hastily undressed, lay down in bed and pulled the covers up to his chin.

"Let me be hungry. Sleep is the Lord's meal." Then he turned and fell silent.

That same night, he awoke suddenly and was fully alert.

He felt his right shoulder, as he could still feel there the pressure of the hand which had shaken him and raised him abruptly from his empty sleep.

"Who's there?" he asked into the darkness in which the light of the full moon lay like a phosphorescent veil.

Nothing.

"Who?" he repeated more urgently and half sat up in bed.

Then he stared for a long time with both eyes boring into the trembling silence.

The longer he sat there and exerted himself, the more tormenting was the certainty that he was cowering lost and alone in an endless, black expanse into which no light, no help could penetrate. All human life too far to call for.

"Alone, all alone, *me*, just *me*", he pondered emptily to himself in idle dullness.

But it had not been an illusion that something had woken him from his night, for he felt in himself a tense hearkening to something.

"Perhaps my heart is packing up and they've come to wake me up because it's time." —

His head fell onto his chest. He drew his knees up and let his soul stare into these thoughts as though into a deep well, motionless and in a cold cramp.

But he found nothing, no end, no resolution.

After a long time it sank again into silence within him, like snow from heavily-laden clouds,

"Who could it be? — Who in heaven do I have on earth who means me well?" —

But he kept the name of his dead wife as a secret to himself. For he was afraid of it driving away the spirit which he now felt more and more distinctly around him.

Cautiously he lay down again, listening and not daring to stir.

"If it's true, it'll come three times", he thought and sensed how the expectation was constricting his chest.

His blood was roaring in his ears like a broad forest.

Didn't something glide along the wall, softly like a swishing dress? — — — — Yes! — — — And steps? — — — No! — — — But yes! — — — Like when a soft breeze rolls a withered leaf across the ground — a soft pecking — — in between a scurrying dragging — past the table — on to the end of the bed — agonising — slow.

With wide eyes he follows the direction of the mysterious sounds.

It is sort of wafting, barely perceptible, and yet his sight is now discerning it exactly, the longer he follows it. In the monotonous, trembling grey around him there is something black, without arms, without legs, without head, bulky like a wall.

In the silent movements, however, lies the gravity of a commanding presence, and now, as a wavering tendency comes over it, he feels like his innermost depths are casting themselves onto their knees stammering.

"Nothing, nothing", he soothes himself and yet feels like his inner being is opening up as though he wants to suck the indescribable shadows into himself in ice-cold hunger.

Then it is finally standing by the edge of his bed, an abyss in the air, motionless.

Held he looks into it, quite powerless, full of anguish. He feels like something nameless is flowing through the trembling beams of his eyes into the dark one waiting there.

It is coming from the most sacred expanses of his soul. With soft-shadowed wings, the night-bird draws away, it fades away like a cloud from the sparkling mirror of a child's eyes. Behind it a pale expanse opens up with a brightly trembling, infinite horizon. In the fearful din of his visible emotion, however, a desire for help was rising, faint and limp.

Then the spectre is gone and the night has soaked it up, completely, with nothing left over, no restive dream remains either.

A cry which loses itself dead tired in an empty expanse, without rousing an echo. That is what the life of the old shingle maker was after his wife's death.

He was not yearning for her so that his days would leap colourfully around him. He was longing for her in the way a fallen tree longs for its roots.

But it was not a protean, polymorphous desire. It weighed over him like a heavy, still mist, so that his years passed like clenched breaths which neither invigorated nor relieved.

He wandered around aimlessly like the wind.

The thoughts were sinking from his soul like the tree letting its wizened needles drop without feeling.

His dreams became desolate.

In the end, it was nothing but walls slowly streaming into each other, lifeless cries, empty noises, mountains bearing down, turbid flight, witless fear.

He was going to bed ill-tempered.

His getting up was an escape.

Often before daybreak, already dressed, he leant on the window and looked wistfully up at the forest. Then, when the first yellow streak smouldered over the mountain, the feeling of certainty would come over him.

But the next morning, it was different. The church bells had already rung out into the valleys. The woodcutters' axes were already tapping from the nearby forest. Old Hannig was already sitting on the bench in front of the house and squinting against the sun.

No sound yet came from the shingle maker's room.

"Ullrich, go and listen at the door, nothing has stirred from that room yet", the woman said to the midget.

He went. After a while, he returned and shook his head while a pleasant smile stretched the thin skin over his pointed face in thread-like creases,

"Seffie, what would you think, if he was dead?"

"Go and see straightaway, dear, go. And he did come home in such a state yesterday."

In happy impatience, the woman poured out these words to the midget who went off again in high spirits.

He softly pushed the door open and peered with long neck into the retiree's room.

The woman had followed him and was looking with rapt curiosity over his shoulder into the little room.

Franz was lying motionless on his back in bed. His eyes were staring at the ceiling. He looked like a dead man. But an animated, astonished joy was playing around his lips.

The midget hesitated.

"Now what is the man looking at?" asked Josepha impatiently, shoving Ullrich to the side and crashing over the threshold. Then the old man jumped in fright and looked dissatisfied at the couple.

"Hey, hey," the woman turned scornfully to her man, "that would be one for dying. He won't be leaving, not before he has devoured the last shingle from the roof. He is sneaky to the bone, I know better."

Ullrich paled. His silent smile was unsightly. With softly quavering words, he answered,

"No Seffie, he isn't dying, he's rotting away in his living body. — Right, Tone, that's what you're doing. — He's already started, smell how it stinks. Pooh, the devil!" and he spat.

It was the venom of this treacly voice which brought the old man to himself again.

"Go, go, I'll get up straightaway", he answered timidly and turned to the wall.

"And quick, Ullrich doesn't have much time. You have to plough the potatoes", the woman commanded him firmly in going. Then the door fell shut loudly behind the couple and Franz climbed cautiously out of bed.

His face assumed the expression of rapt attention again when he saw he was alone. In getting dressed, he paused a few times and pondered to himself.

"What was that thing in the night?" he asked himself and shook his head.

Then he looked under the bed: a few dirty shirts, old shoes and boots to which crusts of dry muck were stuck.

"This isn't working", he pondered.

He tapped tentatively here and there on the wall and checked whether all the windows were shut.

He found nothing suspicious. Nevertheless, he was dead certain that something had happened in the night.

He remembered everything tangibly and distinctly, especially how he had sat in bed and watched the silence and blackness, and how something nameless had flowed out through his eyes' rigid gaze into it, leaving behind a silent relief. The cramp of an inner knot had disentangled itself and his being had flown into the expanse in tired breaths.

As he had gone to sleep, so had he awoken.

Already the morning sunshine was playing with the dust in his room as he opened his eyes.

He did so with complacency. Getting up was as easy for him as if he had consumed a big meal in his sleep. His soul had acquired roots. He stretched as though on a broad firm foundation.

And all that had brought him the silent shadows which had walked towards him that night.

It had also shaken him, it occurred to him, shaken him awake ...

Now, since he was up and thinking about it, the thought occurred to him that he got up in the night.

Only, he had slept so fast and sound!

How could something occur to him like that: to have been fast asleep and have gotten up at the same time.

But the more vehemently he rejected the puzzling contradiction, the more strenuously it returned.

"I'll look into the sun a little, then it'll go away", he thought and gazed out straining into the light while he endeavoured to direct his whole attention onto something. Only, this absurd thought was excluding every sense and dominating his awareness tenaciously. Actually it was not a thought, it was more of a state which filled him distinctly, precisely with an idea. But it was not constant: it transformed itself, fled, pushed forward, melted away into a trembling soft light in the fabric of his soul, merged together like a liberating idea. In all its transitions, its outer edges stayed sharp and clear and its whole being stretched out to him as surely and quietly as he had not felt for a long time.

Now it was floating *across* again and from a vivid rain *into him*, and it felt like the skipping waves of a quick mountain stream, like gleaming gold dust particles that are standing up lightly to dance ... finally: standing. All these scenes were so completely evident to a hidden understanding and so incomprehensible to the old man's alert mind that a hot fear came over him.

Old people go crazy sometimes! — With shaking hand he brushed his grey hair behind his ears. Perhaps he already was! — —

Full of dread, he opened the vest again which he had just buttoned up, tore his dirty shirt apart and stared at his hairy, powerful chest,

"Those are my hairs," he pondered, "here and there a grey one, and there I push my breath in and out in the morning. — — A madman would never know that."

"Good, good", he murmured now contented, turned and left the little room with firm steps.

But when he entered the rooms of his hosts, breathed in the dull smell of boiled turnips, heard the horribly shrill voice of the woman and saw the man skulking about with cautious steps like a spider, then the old lethargy came over him. He sat down softly at the table as always, reached for a potato from the bowl and timidly cut a small piece of butter onto his slice of bread.

But such complete powerlessness was not lying in him as it usually did. A restlessness survived in him, a rising bitterness.

"Man, you're making as happy a face as a trodden down slipper", scoffed the midget who had just sat down at the table opposite him.

"Laugh on my behalf, if you can", the "resurrected" man roared from the depths of his soul, harshly defiant and completely against the will which still lay dull and dormant in him. "Well now?"

The midget recoiled before the old man's primal fury as though before something unheard of.

But when he found his courage again to look at the retiree sharply, inquiringly, the weary old man was already sitting opposite him as always.

A softly twitching tremor was all that betrayed the secretly awoken life in the deep folds of his coarse face.

That face was returning the dwarf's abrasive harshness.

After a short, hidden brooding, he burst out seething, "Now see that you take the cows out!"

Clumsily willed like a docile steer, Franz rose and trotted outside.

"I'll thrash you!" Ullrich called out behind his broad back in fierce daring.

It was seven in the morning when old Franz appeared under the solitary spruce in front of the house with the cows yoked together according to plan.

Just then Ullrich was disappearing behind the first trees of the forest, an axe over his shoulder and a bundle of rope in his left hand. The two gleaming, red-streaked animals pricked their ears, beat lazily with their tasseled tails and bellowed with joy in the pure air still filled with the last of the night chill. The forest reflected the sound cheerfully. Its shadow stretched right up to the path. Only very slowly did it roll back. On the other side of the path, the meadows started which had once been the old shingle maker's inheritance and which he had thoughtlessly given away seven years ago in the drunkenness of his misery. They lay as long, thin stripes in a shallow arc before the forest, but without reaching up to it. A meadow spread itself just as thinly in between as a protective belt in whose short grass lay strewn weathered sandstone boulders and smaller rocks.

The trees of the forest hate the crops of the ploughed fields. They have a bitingly coarse breath. They blow it onto the plants cared for by men, in their face, in their inner leaves, right to their roots so that they remain frail, turn yellow and finally shrivel up without having borne fruit. Yes, the germ in the earth stiffens even unto death before the air of these merciless, sharp needles.

Only the grass sown by the Lord himself is permitted by the trees, so that it plays at their feet and laughs with its garrulous swaying.

Then, probably from curiosity, they dip their enormous branches low to the ground to listen to what the tiny herb men are saying in whispers.

Then the forest often breaks suddenly into thundering laughter over the childish secrets of the little grasses.

It is a wild, blustering sound when the black forest giants laugh with their whole body.

And the white virgin clouds sleeping in their blue heaven's bed are woken by it. A shiver of fright passes through them. Their father, the wind, also jumps up. At first he swirls around upset. Then he takes his frightened daughters by the arm and hurries them, pulling in great leaps so that the delicate clothes of the air-maidens are wafting along after them.

Then quick shadows scurry across the fields on earth. Those are the horrors chasing after the fleeing fearfully. And in the meadows over which they hurry, the timorous blades bend down. When they are past, the blades slowly rise up and then sway their green heads disapprovingly for a while over the sudden disturbance.

After that they stand quite still again. The scared off sun comes out and restores their trust. It tells them of the boon which will someday grow from their hollow stems. The seeds of the field take that warmly to heart so that their joy soars over them in trembling fervour.

This tale of spring was not depressing the old man for the first time in seven years. He stood there in a soft, lustfully bleak rapture and waited for Josepha whom he could hear still crashing about with the empty wooden crockery in the house.

He stood bolt upright behind the cows, turned his chest to the forest and breathed in deep draughts the chill streaming from there. His chest sucked the air in hastily. Then he noticed to his satisfaction that the quiet assuredness which the billowing shadows of the night had brought him was being fetched up by these relieving breaths and flowing into all his senses, bringing an almost forgotten freshness and strength to him.

It was as though a blindfold was falling from his eyes. And everything around him possessed more vivid colours, louder tones, refreshing movements.

He was stimulated by the the air. Soon the cows were standing harnessed to the plough.

Then he impatiently cracked the whip twice and looked over to the door to see if the woman was coming soon.

"Hey!" he called out to her.

How it *rang!*

Then again, "Hey!"

Now he was screaming it.

In the end it was not impatience at all anymore, but an aggressive call. With each of these deep trumpeting blows, a part of the last remnant of that secret prohibition under which he had stood for seven years flew out of him.

And his ear imbibed the colourful echo of his voice as a refreshment for his soul. It was bliss for him, a self-revelation. —

"Old fool! what are you grizzling for? — I'm standing here and you're whinging despite it."

The woman was standing right at the head of the righthand cow. She now grasped its halter and pulled on it, "Now, gee!"

But Franz was still standing silently under the power of self-awareness.

"You, Seffie," he said in proud joy, "call again", and his face shone.

"Fool!" the woman yelled furiously.

A shrill, weak sound lost itself among the trunks of the forest.

But, "Up!" thundered the shingle maker with all his lungs.

And its echo returned arrow-quick. It came across the feeble, inimical echo like a swishing punch and laid it out on the ground halfway.

"Yes, yes!" the powerful greyhead straightened and looked at her in the pride of victory, but without budging. Josepha succumbed. It was a battle which their spirits were contending. But then a senseless fury overcame the woman. She kicked the animals' bodies with her feet so that they drew up in pain.

In sudden defiance, the retiree seized the plough and, with enormous strength, tore the team completely from the floundering woman,

"Ha, ha, Seffie, you never got anywhere with me until I let you!"

Then he tolerated, smiling, the whole list of rude names which she impotently said under her breath.

Finally he cracked the whip.

"Now, gee!"

The cows walked in regular, unhurried steps. The plough dug clanking through the stony, sandy soil and threw the dirt up by the young potatoes.

For two furrows, everything went smooth and steady. With the third, the woman, angry over her defeat, began nagging. Now it was going too slow for her, now too quick, now too far to the right, now too far to the left; now Franz was tearing the earth too deep, now too shallow.

Then the shingle maker could no longer hold his fury. He belted the cows so that they ran like wild. The woman tried to stem the haste with all her bodily might. She was dragged along. Her cries turned into shrill weeping. But it was as though Franz was drunk. His large eyes were blazing. With fierce strength, he was lashing the plough's draught animals constantly on the legs, inciting them more and more. They were covering themselves with sweat. The woman was staggering limply behind them.

With a jerk, he finally stopped them and dried his moist brow with his big, brown hand.

Josepha threw him a venomous look.

"Now, Seffie, no, no! I don't have to if I don't want to, take note", he answered.

Then he did his work steadily and quietly to its end, led the cows into the barn, bound into his handkerchief his slice of bread, which had turned out this time to be smaller than usual, grasped his stick and left the house.

In front of his neighbour's house, his friend, old Hannig, was sitting on a wooden bench. He was an old man. In his yellow, puffy face, a fat nose was stuck, short and blue like a ripe plum. He was filling it awkwardly and painstakingly full of snuff and offered the approaching shingle maker a pinch as he finished that business, so as to then immediately begin his unending chat, "A June like no one could have wished for, warm and beautiful."

Franz usually sat for hours chatting next to his neighbour. Today he found it painful to see his old comrade blathering breathlessly and at the same time waggling his white head comically.

In the soft air encompassing these wilted men, Franz was sensing within himself a youthful superiority. "True", he thought to himself and fell silent while he snorted the tobacco.

"Have you had an argument with them? It sounded like it, am I right?"

"Argument", the shingle maker repeated out of boredom.

And then succinctly, "Farewell, friend!" With that he went.

Hannig looked at him uncomprehendingly.

"A funny guy, Franz Tone! Ha, ha, ha, ha!" and he ejected his snidely grumping coughs. "And always in spring, around the time of sprouting, as if the sap was still niggling him. Ha, ha, ha!" —

For how could he have known that the shingle maker's lost life had come back to him? It manifested itself as an urge to call out loudly, to make long, firm strides, as a freely wandering gaze. Franz was raising his stick higher than usual and thrusting it down more stridently.

It was suffusing him like flickerings, like the billowing of detached walls.

Hermann Stehr

When, after half an hour, he was again sitting on his hard beam and cutting broad, curly shavings from the wood with his whittle as the pale light and the loneliness of the barn surrounded him, he became calmer and thought of how it all came about that the life had awoken in him once more deep down in his soul.

Nothing but spring had brought it.

Always when the spring storm had torn the winter mist from the wreath of the distant mountain and the blue vastness of the expanse beckoned with its blurred lines through the deep pass, the calm, a deep anguish had inexplicably risen in him in the place of the steady dullness. But it had always remained a feeble digging in the sad affairs of his undeserving situation. His procrastination, his timid anger had only been born anew.

He was probably feeling in May the new freshness going through his body. Only this strength was then burdening him like a niggling acknowledgement of his impotence.

"Ha, you're weakening, scrawny body, how you panted. My strength is just a pack of misery for me."

For no liberating resolution was pulling it together, no plan was guiding it. The wanting, hoping, colourfully contending life had been placed in the grave with his wife. His masculine spirit had fled from his body with that hot breath of horror when he had found his wife dead in bed.

Sitting there dully and waiting for death.

But the choking had arrived more fervently this spring. An occurrence had shown that especially clearly.

On a Sunday morning he had looked out his small window at the path. During the full twelve hours of the day almost nobody walks up and down it. But it grants the pleasure of observing the half smudged footprints in the sand of the path. You can make up all kinds of stories about them.

In this way, he was looking out at the path and reading the tracks lying in it. Actually, he was not doing it voluntarily, but rather something in his soul had said to him that if he were to look out into the greenery, "into life", into the light, then he would lose the feeling of invisible fists pressing into the back of his head.

He effortlessly saw a tale.

In the middle of the path, carelessly flopped in the deepest sand, broad and hulking, there lay traces like that of a keg pressed into the ground. Behind them, always stopping at equal intervals, followed a long, narrow footprint and a hollow which had been dug by clenching toes.

Haha, his thoughts addressed the crude footprints, little fisherman, you're also thinking that the Lord lets a bush grow forever like in heaven. Well yes, yes! — But, why do you need to steal like a giant from the pines, running with your legs apart? —

You could have gone twice. To the woman, stepping on the tree tops, it would be too heavy though with your wild paws. — — — — — Then a tangle of delicate, youthful sounds rang out disruptively from the mountain. They quickly swirled closer and already four girls' colourful skirts were flitting around the corner.

"Now I'm going to cook, that sand looks like white flour."

The children were swirling around each other jubilantly, all caught-up in their joy and not noticing the old man.

Soon the offices are distributed. A girl of about seven years beats sweet butter in the dust with a stick, a roly-poly little one smears the cake tin, while she streaks a number of stones carefully with her hand. A third assembles the dough in a deep wheel track.

The homemaker, the blond nestling from Hannig's house, sits on the edge of the field, her hands folded idly on her white apron, a sweet gravity on her innocent, glowing face. Her deep-blue eyes watch in sparkling joy.

How she twitters and laughs and scolds and speaks sagely ... But the shingle maker's heart does not rise with the sight of this charming picture. The appearance of the children was repugnant to him, and yet he was now looking raptly attentive at every grasp of those small hands, at every step of those swift little feet — and yet, at the same time, his unease was growing into anguish. Running out, wanting to grasp a hide and shake — shake — shake — so that — that. — Finally it became unbearable for him and his scream rumbled harshly amongst the raptly playing children so that they leapt away hurriedly.

But when the path now lay deserted again and nobody was playing on it except the quiet light of the sun, he felt his dreariness, his loneliness, his sorrow more deeply than ever before. —

That image of playing children stayed in him like a bright radiance.

On this sparkling backdrop, his brooding was picturing with lustful bitterness, with painful exactness, all the hardness, lovelessness and neglect with which his hosts had injured his life. And when he was finished, he did not just laugh stupidly as usual. No, his sorrows raised themselves out of their long, dull rest and began to push for a way out.

With a thousand assailing little voices, his splintered, tormented soul was crying impotently for an end.

And spring brought him the solution.

As the sun had climbed higher, the clouds had flown further; as the world had decorated itself more colourfully and the birdsong had sounded more and more ardent, a closed off yearning finally released itself for the first time from the lifeless debris of his inner being. The previous evening on the way home, he had screamed it spluttering to the stars in heaven. — —

It was all rolling around in the old man's inner vision as a stream of misunderstood images whose content and linkages he was experiencing as a mood working its way up increasingly into the light of a restful peace.

He had already stopped working a long time before. His arms propped stiffly on his legs with splayed fingers, he was sitting motionless in the barn on his hard beam and staring with wide eyes at the clutter of shavings.

The farmer was walking then through the yard across to the half-open barn door. When he saw the shingle maker sitting there so motionless, he crept in and leant gently against the barn's wall.

"Now I'll just see how long this lasts!" he thought.

Suddenly Franz abruptly rose up and hastily grasped the whittle. When he saw Kroner, he looked at him for a long time with his still dreamily staring face. Then he began to smile in mysterious joy, whilst nodding meaningfully and firmly.

Finally it came out slowly, still laden with all his emotion,

"Yes, yes, Kroner, look at me, I'm now another man, I'm living again — last night death went past me like a black towel, silent as a wall. And either I have to go behind it or all is well." —

His returned life manifested itself to the shingle maker thus: through the tales of spring, it had flown over his raised shoulders as a rope-strong calm; it had answered his storming cry with a jubilant echo which had shaken him fully awake; and finally, for the first time in so many years, a furious masculine will had found its way into the decayed mines of his strength to detonate them in a wild act. Josepha's fury had been changed suddenly into impotent weeping before his snorting laughter.

It had all surged on a thousand hidden paths from the lonely yearning to die which had ambushed him on the way home. It was also dripping from the countless wounds received in his cowering state. He was now experiencing that long-lasting, undeserving condition as though muffled in cotton wool.

In the first joy of his reawakening, he forgot entirely that he was still sick.

In the evening, Franz Tone went home with the sinking sun, as always. He was not carrying his dry bread crusts home again in the red handkerchief as usual. In lip-smacking leisure, he had consumed the hard crusts for lunch. That wild unease, that billowing of detached walls had disappeared entirely from him. His stride was back to normal, only somewhat longer and steadier. His head was bowed gently forward as though searching, not hanging limply anymore. His eyes were sparkling in uniform, broad beauty. A transfiguration lay in the deep creases of his rough face.

He was walking thus, heedless to everything else. His senses were looking at the many colours within him, the light. And as he paused, intending to walk around a bend, he noticed that the village path was clogged up with playing children. They were moving in circles and singing,

> Florian, Florian,
> Lay for seven years.
> Seven years are over,
> Florian rolls over.

He did not find himself attempting at once to go past as usual with an angry grumble, but paused, covered by the low branches of a plum tree, and watched with interest the seesawing circling of the children.

In the meantime, the day was expiring in a blissful swoon. The shadows were eagerly weaving ever heavier veils. There in front of him on the path, the little ones were dancing in sweet monotony and singing the song of the revived Florian to the sinking sun. His attentiveness changed into dazed emotion.

Florian rolls over!

The children hollered it one last time in high spirits, clutched each other, gave each other jokingly the "last one" and disappeared into the surrounding houses from which they had already been called, through the tangled branches of the fruit trees. And all was completely silent. Over the forest, the night was awakening.

Franz started from the bonds of a resolve whose domination had sprung up deep in his soul through the children's song. Mechanically he fell into his regular stride. When he crossed the place where the children had been dancing, he paused involuntarily and looked around in circles. With that he shook his head and smiled to himself full of satisfaction. "The children don't know everything. — Yes, but they don't realise it.

That only comes later. For what man likes vinegar in his youth?"

Then he walked onwards again, but his collected poise showed that the initial thoughts were driving deeper, binding themselves more and more with all that was dormant in him.

Between the first mountain house and the village which, already shrouded in mist, lay to the left of his feet, he paused again.

The growing resolve was working its way up into clarity. — — — — — — "Florian, Florian, lay for seven years" ... See, Tone, it all tallies. — "Seven years are over" ... too. — "Florian turns over" ... no, not that: turns over and lies on his left side, what he had borne on his right. — — — — — Perhaps under the spruce those two are thinking ... But pay attention! — Florian gets up, puts a clean shirt on, walks into a swept room, looks out a clean window, eats when he's tired and sleeps in a clean bed like seven years ago, like he lay down."

He said all that in those vague murmurs with which the deepest thoughts ring out from us. It sounded so gentle because it was already spoken when his strength first gathered in the core of his will. Then he climbed lustily onwards, soothed, as though he had only now finished his work.

For his soul had also finally finished a day's work which he had longed for with his dull sorrow, his bitterness and prickling frailty. The higher he went, the warmer the air became, as if he was overtaking the stream of fervent human prayers on their way to the Father.

The starless expanse of the summer night filled with broken voices above, like scattered stammering.

Nothing on earth gave an answer, other than the cautious dream-swishing of the sleeping forest.

The shingle maker found the house door open, but everything appeared to be lying in deepest peace.

He knocked on the door of his hosts because he recalled that yesterday he had also come about supper time, "Seffie! — Seffie! — Ullrich!"

Nobody answered. A turn of the door handle, a repeated call also remained to no avail. Only he thought he could hear a quite quiet giggling once it had become completely still around him.

"She's laughing. Let it be."

He said it with deliberate calm and went into his room.

"My, my ... and then." —

With a confident smile, he expressed his resolve once more into the dull night before going to sleep.

Before sunrise, in deep darkness, Franz arose, quickly put his Sunday clothes on without looking around and hastily left his room.

He spent the time before breakfast outside.

Ullrich went past him, pushing the barrow before him in which the gleaming scythe lay. The midget was going to get fodder and did not deign to look at him. The old man watched him indifferently. The woman was scurrying in and out and acting as though he did not exist at all to her.

That did not disturb him.

After an hour, he entered the large living room with steady stride behind the man returning home, greeted him calmly and sat down at his usual place.

The couple made gestures of displeasure at him. The shingle maker, however, met their hostile looks with such peaceful eyes that they were confused. They left the room and did not surface again for a long time.

Franz made himself comfortable, smiling deliberately, hung his cap on the wall hooks, unbuttoned his coat and rested against the table.

After a while, the woman peeked hastily through the door. When she saw the retiree still sitting there demurely, she threw him a threatening look and immediately disappeared again, slamming the door shut at the same time.

Quarter hour after quarter hour elapsed.

The pot of potatoes began to whistle. The water in another vessel was overflowing fitfully.

Franz did not yield or waver.

Finally they both reappeared.

After they had walked around the room a few times aimlessly, the woman took the potatoes and the water for the coffee from the stovetop.

"What are you doing there, woman?" Ullrich asked with simulated astonishment.

"Well, I'm putting everything away. I'm not hungry, I had too much yesterday."

"I don't want to eat either", the man parroted his memorised speech.

"But I do!" the old man suddenly thundered, belting his fist on the table and springing up.

"Here, my dinner, here, an hour and a half I've been waiting for it. Now that's enough", he added threatening after a while and took a step unflinchingly into the room after the couple.

"Give it to him! ... Give it to him!" the midget burst out in fearful confusion at his boldly irate wife, who was already beginning to tremble with fury again. He whirled around the room, raising his pointed shoulders in comical indignation and throwing timid looks at the old man who was still standing fast, his fists propped stiffly on the table.

"... give it to him ... give it to him ... give it to him", Ullrich repeated continuously in helpless impotence. But when he saw that Franz had sat down peacefully again, a fierce courage came over him. He ran over to him, spat in front of him and shouted, forgetting his soft, gentle ways completely, screaming hoarsely,

"Here ... here — ... yes ... give it to him ... to him, to him ... Ugh! Disgusting!"

Then he vacated the room quickly for the sake of safety.

The woman watched him alone and did not dare to resist him anymore. She shoved the food contemptuously towards the waiting man. At the door, however, her fury overwhelmed her. She turned around and laughed in shrill derision,

"Haha! — means nothing to me! — Such an old toddler — — — in a Sunday suit — — — and on a weekday — — — mph! — mph! — pounding away too, well now, now — — dear Lord! — — who are you courting?"

She was forgetting all caution. With each of her excited exclamations, she took a step closer. Now she was standing right in front of the heedlessly eating retiree.

"Who are you courting?" she repeated shaking with fury. "You beater, show me your contract that ..."

But she could not complete it.

Lightning quick Franz sprang up and seized her tightly by the wrist.

"Ullrich! — Jesus Maria! — Help!"

Like a feather, her man flew in and, whilst springing wildly back and forth, he screamed threateningly,

"What? what? what? — Let her go, I say! Let her go, I say! — What, do you want my wife ..."

"Shut up, you — — crybaby!"

With imperious rudeness, full of scorn, the shingle maker cut off the coward's speech and at the same time gently let go of Josepha's hand.

After that he looked from one to the other smiling mildly and silently, for some time, and his gentle soul composed itself after the storm of indignation. With an amiably thoughtful nod of his head, he prefaced the following, "Oh! — well,now! — Are you stupid! — Franz Tone, the old shingle maker who has never produced a child, hit yourself, Seffie, now, is under your heart another already softly beginning to beat? — Not with love! No, but it's true, I'm no sapling, but a willow wand also breaks. — — So, enough for now. The rest can wait till midday. I'll be here at twelve for lunch. — — And now, in God's name, on the double!"

With solemn steps, the old man left the room without once looking back.

Astonished, thoughtful, the man and woman remained in place for a while.

"What are you thinking now, Ullrich?"

"Haha ..."

"Yes!"

"Hm, hm. —"

"You are a fool, and you know it."

"And you?"

Thus they struggled against the fear that the quiet gravity of the old man had brought over them. After that they each silently took up their usual work.

It was probably after an hour when Ullrich abruptly broke off from his activities,

"You," he shook his wife by the shoulder, "our man is crazy in my opinion."

"If you're right then it'll be a lustful frenzy that puts a quick end to it. But with an old man, where would the lover come from. He seems to me to be far too well", she finished vexed.

They left despondently.

The people in the high mountains are playing a game of dice when they work their fields. Sometimes late frosts occur with early spring, sometimes winter comes too early, sometimes too late. But when the reaped grain first lies whole on the stubble, one of those constant downpours arises which are so common in heavily forested areas.

The only ways out in times of often recurring hardship are hunger or money.

That's why in these solitary cottages so near to heaven, they weep over a lost fifty pfennig piece for weeks. When a child lets the pfennig for buying chicory slide so carelessly from his little hand on his way to the shop, so that it hastily hides itself away between the stones never to be seen again, then his father and mother will beat him mercilessly, and his siblings will watch from the side disapprovingly for a long time as though a heavy stigma adhered to him.

Once, however, a taler piece was lost in a family. The people over the whole mountain spoke of the "misfortune". That family's father became dangerously ill. Weeks later he rose from his bed again. But he was broken. It placed a listlessness over him as though he had suffered an irreplaceable loss. Most of the time, he remained silent as though exhausted, suffering exclamations became his conversation, "Oh, well now!" — "Now, now!" — "Lord, you think so!" — "God, God!"

Only when he came to speak of his lost taler, did his whole being change.

He was always waiting to be able to talk about it. He let everything else pass him by emptily.

But then he would straighten up out of his depression, his eyes would begin to shimmer, his arms would be waving busily through the air. Sometimes he would stand stiff and rigid in the sitting room and moan out the story of his horror, then he would hunker down again and murmur inconsolably about the eternal loss.

Usually he would break off here, take his pipe, which had gone out on him, from the table with trembling hand and go home deeply shaken.

But the Lord God pitied his sorrow.

Once the poor man led a lost person in the deep forest onto the right path. Because the rich gentleman carried nothing smaller on his person, he presented his guide with a shiny taler.

Silent, trembling, as though on tiptoes, in the night, timidly, he walked home. Shaking with silent joy, he sat on the bench and his unhinged soul dared not stir.

When he had convinced himself that all the children were sleeping soundly, he turned the light out. Then he had his distraught wife feel in the hand in which he held the taler.

"A taler?!" she stuttered in joyous confusion.

"A hard ... solid ... taler, my wife! — my wife!! feel it. — God, God!" he replied, breathing ecstatically.

The next morning he lay dead in bed, a blissful smile on his lips, holding the taler tightly with his cold hand.

The joy had killed him.

This pitiable man had been Josepha's father. She had inherited the ardent love of money from him. But she did not go around calmly like he did. Her disposition had elevated this weakness to a passion, to a stinginess as sharp as a knife, as prickly as a thorn. She was constantly scream-ing shrilly as though they were always besieged by thieves who had to be driven away by loud yells.

Now she was optimistic.

This condition, which influences the woman's being so deeply, made her stinginess fiercer, greedier, more ruthless.

And her man, whom nature had denied every power, submitted to this addiction.

Stretching, like certain types of caterpillars, he crept around, soundless as a reptile, with cloying, skulking eyes.

When his nervelessness suddenly changed into pleasure, then the loud nagging of his wife seemed like a caning which brought his obliging avarice to new exaltation. Resolutions and plans were then squirming hidden in his soul, cold as the scrawny bodies of hungry snakes.

Old Franz walked, led by his increasingly ir-reversible resolve, straight to Kroner, the farmer.

"Give me my wages," he said artlessly, "I'm not working anymore today, and from Thursday next week, don't count on me."

"Well now, you have your Sunday best on. Why then on a Thursday?"

"Well, it works out better, it's exactly half the week", Franz answered evasively. But then, as if ashamed of his hesitation, he added quickly and too loud, "Wednesday is my birthday, then things'll change."

"Yes, you mean the Ullrich affliction?" Kroner threw in doubting.

"Yes, and with all of it."

"Ha, old man, if it were true as well. You won't reckon up though!"

"Kroner! ... Farmer! ..."

The shingle maker's words rang out like an eruption. But no ferocity upset the steady calm of his attitude.

"Yes, yes," Kroner appeased him, "I know you, everyone in the village ... but, but ... well, you're so steady, there ... eight marks is it?"

"Hm, hm!"

"There you are. — And on Tuesday come and fetch your birthday present from me. — God be with you! Good luck with your business, good old man!"

"Thank you very much. God be with you."

Then he left. No doubt over the success of his plan arose in him.

With a quiet smile of certainty, he strode up the mountain again.

L unch was over. The old shingle maker wiped his knife clean of potato residue on the table, tested the edge slowly with his thumb, looked inquiringly in his hosts' faces, pondered again for a while, gazing along the knife edge, then let the blade snap sharply into its casing, stuck the knife in his vest pocket, shoved the empty dishes away from himself, propped both elbows firmly on the table and began with a rough, "Well!"

Ullrich and Josepha observed Franz's strange behaviour amusedly, laughing fitfully through their noses, prodding each other under the table with their feet and then sitting completely still in comical seriousness. The midget drew his eyebrows halfway up his forehead to prove his mastery to Josepha.

"You have now been on the mountain seven years", the shingle maker inserted.

"Oh, no, surely not that many!" Ullrich interrupted him in derisory wonder.

"... you have, however, what ..."

"Ullrich, laugh too, laugh, laugh ... hoho, hahaha!" Josepha piped in-between, and the thin man neighed back obediently.

"... not what on the nail there ..."

"Show me what you have in there!" and Ullrich peered at the old man's hand.

The shingle maker lowered his head silently. His breathing was beginning to become audible.

"The man is wearing his Sunday best, Seffie, so he can play Hannig's girls' bogeyman", Ullrich filled out the pause.

"Shut up, don't you see that the old father will flare up", his wife reproached him and inflated her cheeks as a sign of her indignation.

Now the old man raised his eyes again. They had narrowed slightly. He fixed them on the couple and smiled coldly and deliberately.

Changing his plan, he began again in a businesslike manner. But his words came out as though stumbling over an obstacle,

"Bring the purchase agreement here!"

"He wants a purchase agreement. Go dear! My blessed God, Jesus, Jesus, a purchase agreement, to experience such a thing. Quick dear, fetch it, quick, quick! I'll yet die in sorrow."

The woman was wringing her hands as though her greatest fear had come over her.

"Yes, woman, quick."

Like a ball, Ullrich flew to the wall, tore an old, crumpled newspaper from the board stuck up there, and spread it out in front of the shingle maker.

"Here, esquire, Mr Anton Franz of Eschberg in Kaltenbach."

He pushed himself forward obligingly by the old man and made one droll bow after the other. Franz pulled back the knee which Ullrich had touched. His eyes were widening, burning. The blood was draining away from the bulges of his low forehead. All his creases burrowed deeper. But he mastered himself with effort.

"Is that really the purchase agreement, Ullrich?" he asked, and his voice softened.

"Yes, sir", the man nodded in fatuous ingenuousness.

"Is that the purchase agreement?"

His question came out with quaking breath.

"Yes — sir — man —" Ullrich stuttered in rising fear and sought to slip past him.

But Franz seized him by the neck.

"Is that the purchase agreement, loudmouth? — You?"

Now his fury had burst the bonds of his patience. Like stones rubbing against one another, his words became loud, turbid, grating.

The midget was making floundering motions to wriggle out from the grasp of the old man. He was staring trembling into his terrible eyes and screaming madly as though he had lost his senses, "Yes — man — the purchase — yes — yes ... argh — — Seffie ..."

Full of loathing, the old man tossed Ullrich aside like a rat so that he flew into the corner by the shelf of pots. A bowl fell to the floor from the impact and shattered. —

Now Josepha realised the terrible seriousness, broke free from her place and tried a break for the door.

The old man stood in her way,

"You're staying here. Who's to blame that it had to come to this? — Play with who you want, but never with me!"

Ullrich had worked himself meanwhile back onto his legs. His lips were flying with rage, his brow was pale as porcelain, his eyes were flickering. Now and then, he went down on his knee as though grounding his rage and emitted a groaning oath.

Her man's cowardice brought Josepha into an ecstatic fury,

"I'd like to smash you in the face, pathetic ponce! There, what are you looking for? — Take the shards and shred the old steer's face!"

With her fists she closed in on the fearful man.

Franz shoved her away.

"Stay where you are, both of you", he said threateningly, striding to the table and throwing his money on the plate.

"Here! — the eight marks."

"You can see that soon", Josepha said quickly appeased and threw a glance at the midget behind the old man's back as if to say, 'But you were right, he is mad'. Moving up to the table, she added,

"You don't need to sell a man short. — ... one, two, three", she began to count after a while, tapping the coins with her index finger. "It's right!" and she went to sweep the sum up, because she assumed in all seriousness that the "monkey" was so confused that he was ready to atone for his hardness in this way.

But Franz shoved her greedy hand away and looked at her shaking his head.

"Stop! I didn't mean it like that, dumb woman!"

Then he straightened up to his full height. A deep, solemn gravity sank like a veil over the coarse features of his face. Bare rocky mountains look as awe-inspiring when evening is strewing its first sunlit mists over the silent acerbity of their cracks.

And the stone-grey wrinkles commenced with grumpy ceremony,

"That stingy man is also a drunkard: his schnaps is his money. That he understands. —

If I hadn't committed my business to you, it could have been that you would still have old Femfe as farm girl and the old oxen — fool."

The insulted couple were fiercely stirred. But Franz hushed them and continued,

"Good, good! — it's over ... over ..."

Then, without wishing, his voice ran out. A weakness that could not be conquered, the fool's shame, came over him with that thought. Just for one moment. But then he righted himself on the staff of his born-again inner strength,

"The eight marks is for four days, calculated from this Saturday. On Tuesday you are done. Until then I set the times, Seffie. Put everything in order in my room, wash my floor, the blankets, the dirt from the walls, the spiderwebs from the windows, and do my laundry.

It must change, everything, everything, everything!

I was sleeping — was dying — was dreaming ... what do I know? — I recalled that I have also, in a few eyes, suffered like a misty-eyed fellow, like a dazed fool — — and then — — — I awoke and looked around. There I lay, an old ass in the trash in the corner. —

Everything goes up and down ... but still ... for once ... Wednesday is my birthday ... then everything must change ... must? ... must?! ... mu—u—st!!" —

The shingle maker had been speaking in paragraphs, stammering initially, then trembling with the impetus of his last desire.

Now, shaken by the confession of his desperate situation, he looked testingly at the couple. He was shaking from the stress like an incurable patient who has taken his last refuge in poison and is now sitting in bed with large, terrified eyes and waiting with beating heart for it to take effect.

But Ullrich and Josepha had hearts that had cooled long ago under their regular selfishness. They answered his searching gaze with scorn in their embarrassed faces. Their souls remained hidden.

That's why, daunted by the couple's obstinate resistance, he began by lapsing into a beseeching style,

"Look, Seffie — Ullrich — you are children to me — — I beg you, be good to me. Don't behave like rogues. Now leave the insults and arguments at the door. You pool it there going in and out. Look, how it was before ... when my wife ..."

He broke off faltering, powerless. His face was sagging in horror.

The woman smiled assuaged: he is crazy then.

The old man was staring in helplessness: oh, it's all in vain, they're still laughing at you.

Just for a moment. Then a savageness came over him,

"Hm—m—m ...", a seething grumbling. "Ha!" he tore his head upwards in desperate fury. "Dammit! — God won't punish me — you want the whip, like dogs. Good, you shall get the whip.

I won't come in the house until Tuesday. After that, if it isn't all as I've said ... look at the shards on the floor, it'll all end up like that, or I'm not Franz Tone."

With trembling hand, he skimmed the money from the table and walked out wordlessly with thundering steps.

"He's crazy", the woman laughed afterwards.

"Well, just like I said", Ullrich affirmed with satisfaction.

Above the house, where the first bushes of the forest stood in the meadow, three boulders crouched in motionless, eternal plumpness. Two smaller ones to the right and left, a larger one in the middle. Their grey bodies, from whose deep cracks hung moss and here and there even little tufts of a fine-stemmed grass, were thrust deep into the ground.

The shingle maker steered his steps towards the larger one. He stood silently at its foot, as though deliberating. It was to him as though his thoughts had received a brutal, unforeseen jolt and been thrown from the straight road of his plans so that neither the old, steady rhythm, nor the old direction could be recovered. He did not know at all why he was standing by the stone, looking up at it and waiting. Yet ... yet an urge surfacing dreamlike had driven him here: something would come down to him there. So he stood and waited. But it did not come.

That's why he climbed up and sat himself so that the whole wavy plain down below was lying before him. And he waited ... but it did not come over him anymore.

He had wanted to speak to his hosts with soft, friendly words. He had anticipated its carrying out would be like the sweet bliss of a song about the blessed virgin. But he now saw the ferocity, which the scorn of his hosts had whipped him up to, as the confirmation of his failure.

And then those angrily pale faces with their hidden scorn! That softly pricking laughter of the midget which he had heard ringing out indistinctly behind him!

The images inside him were still standing firm. But he was feeling a vortex next to them, it was lying like a worn out veil over them, like a sickly glow which flowed trembling around everything so that the outlines of his thoughts and hopes were blurring.

"Oh no," he consoled himself, "that's just the hustle", and he remained waiting.

The glow of the sun was still moving towards the third afternoon hour. He was thirsty. He stayed where he was.

Stonemasons returning home shouted to him. He gave the appearance of sleeping and did not stir.

With ardent patience, he defeated his hunger. Hoping, he watched the shadows of evening nestling into the valley. Finally the sweetly confiding evening peal of bells carried a beguiling reassurance into his flooded inner being.

He quickly left his elevated seat. He sensed that it was impossible for him to throw a glance at the solitary house under the spruce. The wavering might then begin in him again.

That's why, very quickly, with hurrying steps, he carried his hoard of weak certitude into the valley.

Would he sleep in the forest? He knew where the key to the worker's hut in the depths of the forest lay.

Would he walk to Wangendorf?

Would he spend the night in the village tavern?

Would he wander around in the humid night until morning?

He could also have spent the night with an old friend.

Musing, he strode down to the village and did not notice that it was already becoming pitch-black around him.

Then a beam of light stretched at chest height in front of him through the thick night fog like a thin, shimmering bowstring.

He recoiled as though before a fixed barrier. To the right, seemingly far-off, a red patch of light was swimming, dissolving into thousands of rays. Branches were weaving a tangled braid of shadows in front of it and absorbing its trembling threads except for the one drawn to him through the thick darkness.

Countless particles of dust were dancing around it. They closed in on it hostilely, as though they wanted to suck it away. Here and there, its delicate fabric had already been gnawed away by them. From time to time, it disappeared completely. But it always reappeared and worked itself trembling through the fog.

As he was looking at it, a similar process was taking place in his inner being. From the swirling play of his futile doubts, a resolve was arising mechanically. It was not flowing in any way from a firm intent. His vague will was radiating it indifferently through the denatured enfeeblement of his existence.

Could he do anything smarter moreover? No hand was covering his eyes.

"I'll just have to stay in the village", the shingle maker thought idly.

At that moment behind the branches, a door was flung open above. Steps scuffled out. Then he heard a deep voice,

"Dammit, the schnaps tastes sweet — the window's like you're in a sack, what?"

"Yes, a genuine dry March fog", came the crowing answer.

"You've won something before, ha?"

"Oh," blustered the high voice, "when Semma Thadees didn't come to the party with a smiling king, then I pulled in all the small change. —

Dammit, if only it were here today! I'd be like a hen sitting on it!"

"No, mustn't lose it", the bass replied laughing broadly.

Then the door was closed again behind the heavy steps. And the old shingle maker was all alone again with the pitiful threads of light in the still air.

"Confound it," he finally flared up angrily, "I am a handsome fellow. What will happen if I have to take it seriously on Wednesday, when I'm standing there amidst such stupidity and don't know where to turn. Of course I'll have to stay at the tavern."

And he was already at the signpost leading through the orchard to the tavern.

When he entered, the three gamblers, the only guests, rose.

"Here too?" — "Good evening!" — "The fog has no doubt driven you in too, hasn't it Tone?" they all spoke to him at once.

He answered as well as he could and sat down carefully at an unilluminated table.

The innkeeper, looking like a frog walking upright, placed a light in front of him. Franz put it out again and ate in darkness his dry slice of bread with the piece of jelly he had ordered. After he had drunk some schnaps, he whispered in the innkeeper's ear if he could stay overnight.

"Do you want a bed?"

"What'll it cost?"

"Fifty pfennigs."

From the illuminated table, the crowing one called out curiously, "What's going on that you have to whisper?"

"Now, Franz Tone wants ..."

The shingle maker seized the innkeeper by the hand with such fright that the innkeeper broke off quickly and lied laughing, "He is confessing to me."

"You won't hear much to atone for", opined the cheerful bass.

"Good", the old man began again even softer than before. "Where is it?"

"In the loft. You'll find it well enough."

"I thought so."

After a while, when the gamblers were arguing shrilly over something, Franz crept unnoticed to bed.

He awoke deep in the night.

A comfortable weariness was rippling through his limbs. He stretched out cosily.

Suddenly he leapt up as though something nasty had seized his thoughts.

"Is someone there who is planning something big?" he thought incensed. "Whoever lies weak, remains weak."

He left the bed immediately, clothed himself scantily, went into the barn and lay down there in the hard straw.

Hermann Stehr

Enfeebled, the day had gone to sleep. Sickly it rose. It lay motionless over the mountains, veiled in white vestments. Infinitely tired it raised its face from the rumpled pillows of night's shadows, looking wide awake in its gleaming paleness. And a soundless fevered breath was coming from it, spreading suffocatingly over the earth. The earth was cowering at its feet and looking up to it in mute craving. How sad the earth was, which yesterday had yet been laughing so with pert morning winds. Its lightest thoughts, the birds, were cowering as though in fear. They probably began to sing, but broke off abruptly.

In the distance, the bells were then heaving. —
When you suffer pains that no hero can bear,
no scream can grasp, you do well in dull despair
to begin to push a light song with hot breath
through your gritted teeth. Then wavering tones
emanate. With a breath, they are introduced,
with a breath, they are finished. In between lies
long pauses of mad muteness.

Thus, through the heights, the morning song
of the feverish day chimed, a lullaby of defense-
lessness. —

Even dew didn't fall last night", the innkeeper said to the shingle maker opposite him during breakfast.

"Even dew didn't", the shingle maker repeated dully like an accusation against fate and stopped chewing.

That empty, disconsolate rigidity which had lain over him for seven years was surrounding him again,

'Oh, they did nothing for me, nothing' ... it was creeping lazily over the bleak plans of his consciousness.

"You were no doubt too hot in bed?" the innkeeper kept chattering.

But the old man's entire attention was riveted in cold ardency to his inner being, 'And what after that ... yes, yes?' — and he nodded at the certainty of his disappointment.

"Yes, yes!" he repeated out loud and looked hard at the man opposite.

"Well," the innkeeper said, taking it as an answer, "you need not pay anything then either."

"Amounts to *nothing*, you're right", he continued in the swirl of his sovereign grief. "But ...

but ..." He wanted to be threatening, formidable and ferocious, and yet it was only a cry of pain. The wounds of the embarrassment which he had received in his cowering state lay around his soul like a net peppered with thousands of needles.

He sprung up abruptly so that his chair tipped over crashing.

"I well know, you, I well know. But ... but ..."

"Ha, Tone, what's come over you?" But the spasms of his outraged thoughts did not ease up.

"Florian rolls over! ... no! no!" he laughed hoarsely. "Florian gets up, gets up!" and he began striding around the room excitedly.

"But Tone!" the innkeeper said reproachfully and caught him by the arm.

"Yes, yes, innkeeper, you're right."

He came to his senses and looked about with frightened eyes. But then his raw grief suddenly burst out once more,

"What's too much is too much. I won't take it anymore!"

Now the innkeeper knew everything.

"Come," he send distracting him, "don't let the coffee get cold. Don't get angry. It won't change anything."

"No, my appetite is gone", the old man warded him off.

"Well, you put a jacket on, then come with me to the church. It'll be eight soon. Before I get to Wangdorf it'll be nine."

"Yes, innkeeper, I'll go with you. I want to let God into my life."

But in the church, he did not find what he was looking for. The pastor preached on the text of Matthew 16:24,

"If any man will come after me, let him deny himself, and take up his cross, and follow me."

The shingle maker sat there lost and listened to the words of toleration, acquiescence in the will of God, of forgiveness and charity. They shoved him back into his unbearable yoke. God shall bless him and turn him away.

"But God is faithful, who will not suffer you to be tempted above that ye are able" spoke the pastor.

"But it doesn't end, doesn't end, and I'm not taking it anymore", the shingle maker answered to himself.

The clergyman was continuing to exhort to a self-abasement with his mournfully singing voice. The sermon was emerging monotonously from the slow flow of his weak thoughts, like a sluggishly bursting bladder. The congregation was dozing off. In the rays of light hanging from the windows like a luminous giant fan slanting into the sacred dawn, the dust was playing airily, foolish words of man in eternally living light.

The old man became more and more restless.

He coughed and blew his nose to divert his agitation. The soft whimpering was flowing gently from the pulpit — — — and again, "If any man will come after me ..."

The shingle maker was fishing in his pockets and looking for something. He was barely able to stand it anymore.

It was as though he was being mocked, and exposed as an angry man in front of the whole congregation. Oh, and "they" were there perhaps too. These sweet words were sanctifying their hate and encouraging their squalid meanness ... Suddenly he began to feel through his whole body the enormous number of small, poisonous wounds to his soul which their tormenting had beaten into him when he had been cowering.

Oh, and these tepidly circuitous words were burrowing around in him like soft threads, an unbearable feeling, so that he had to press his legs together because a need was suddenly engaging itself.

Finally, "Amen."

Feet were rumbling. The sleepers were rising, tearing their eyes open, looking around for a while blindly, then bowing down, yawning at the pulpit, crossing themselves and saying, "In the name of the Father, the Son and the Holy Ghost. Amen."

The shingle maker also snatched his cross to his chest with excited hand, spitting angrily at the same time and thinking, 'He reads from the little book, but he doesn't understand a scrap about life. How could he spout on so stupidly?' — Then he sat soothed in grim pleasure that his resolve still remained despite the sermon. With a thankful genuflexion towards the altar, he finally left the house of God as the last person.

The square in front of him was already empty. Sparrows were hopping idly around on the sand and pecking at crumbs. The sun hung high in the sky in dully seething fervour. A trembling haze lay across the mountains. Distant objects looked oddly drawn-out in it: the trees looked as if they were on tip-toes, the houses looked like they had unnaturally elongated chimneys. In between, as though curled many times in impatience, were the fields.

Far in the distance, the Eschberg looked like the crookedly straining back of a porter on which lay cottage after cottage like misshapen stone heaps: one, two, three ... up to eight. A little to the left of the last one, the boulder next to the black strip, there it was! — — — Over there, behind the pale strips, in the bend of the forest.

Could the windows be seen? — Something white? — They must have already begun the washing long ago, if they wanted to fulfill his wishes.

The shingle maker looked for a white point for so long that his eyes were hurting. But he did not notice anything and, in his soul, a ball of morbid longing, disappointment, hate, trembling and wild indignation was unfurling ... into which a prickling poison was falling ever slower from the wounds ripped open by the sermon, drip by drip.

Meanwhile people were walking up and down the village path, which was also the main road. Goods wagons were creaking along, a carriage rolled past.

Across at the Cantor's house, the laughing tunes of a piano were leaping out a wide-open window. Cows were mooing, dogs were barking.

All these sounds were flowing as a dim hum past his inwardly closed ears.

From time to time, his soul would stare through all his senses with morbid tenseness at the external world; then it would sink back into dull sorrow; then it would coil into fury; then it would rage with every thought, finally standing rigid in dazzling clarity ... but only to pass through the spectrum of paroxysms anew.

He was beginning to lose all control over himself. Through the disappointments of his failed life, his will had turned wild.

Only far off in the expanse of his inner being did a pale region lie in changeless peace, his last well-being. A trembling allure hung over it, like waving, wilted arms, a sky like a sweetly refracting eye. And whilst the robust limbs of his everyday existence were wreathing in poisoned ferocity, all the festive notes of his soul were surging into it in wordless silence.

Spring lights play over the glassy rushing waves of an unfettered stream in the same way.

When he left the church square, he did not know again where to go. A feeling like revulsion deterred him from returning to his village. But what should he do? — —

Walk — — — walk — — to Ringsdorf, the train goes past there. You can wait for the train's arrival and watch who gets off ... You can go to Eisenthal past the blast furnaces ... along the main road and watch the comings and goings, look at the horses ... My God! — my God! Heavens! if I get home and everything is just as before ...

But he was frightened by his ferocity, and he was frightened by the weary restful bliss which the first fright bore ... and ... "I must, I must" ...

Wangendorf lay far behind him, surrounded by fields with quiet ears. The distant haze had descended from the mountains, the hot sky was hanging deeply and had that light grey colour which iron plates have before annealing. The air which old Franz was breathing was like a scalding drink. The rigid mountains were lying in the haze like powerless schemes. Here and there over the blue-green, motionless expanse of grain were bushes, one like a threatening fist, one like a hand waving for help with fingers contorted in pain ... but the leaf-trembling, oppressive fervour lay over everything.

The seething and threatening, the trembling and pleading, the slipping away of every quiet strength was in him and around him. He fled before this martyring condition but encountered it everywhere he turned.

But at least, when he strode in haste, he felt confident in the rough skin of his life force.

So, out of self-defence, he hurried through villages, across meadows, on paths near forests.

Then he headed for busy taverns. In the noise which in its variety drowned out the monotonous cogwheels of his soul, he found peace. Then some word ringing from a neighbouring table tore him up and drove him away again.

He wandered anew.

Sometimes he was surer of success: then he would stroke the cheeks of playing children and give them coins; other times everything seemed to be in vain: then he would drag himself away wearily, always talking softly to himself; other times indignation came over him: then he would be constantly spitting and replying to the greetings of passersby with hoarse laughter.

Quite often he stopped to look at the solitary house on the Eschberg to see if fluttering linen was hanging next to it. He knew clearly that it was pointless looking into the distance through the glowing haze but kept doing so in yearning restful bliss.

Early on Tuesday he rose in Wiedenhof, four miles away.

He asked the landlady, whose long face consisted of distinctive vertical wrinkles, how far it was to Buchdorf.

"A good eight hours. Do you want to go there today?"

He nodded.

"Well, see then that you dress up warm. A storm's coming today, and a bad one."

He paid the landlady and left.

Dark clouds with red-stained edges had emerged from the seething haze. They were almost sitting on the ground. The leaves of the bushes and trees were hanging limply. The swallows were flying low to the ground. The horses on the street were trotting with crooked knees and lowered heads in a cloud of dust and horseflies. When the lazy wagoner spurred them with the whip, they just flapped their tails sullenly without hastening in the least. The finches were emitting long, suffering cries. The humidity was unbearable.

But it spurred him on, and the greater his sweat ran the more he kicked on.

With strong strides he charged to his goal as though with closed eyes and ears.

"I must, I must!"

Just this exclamation. It was everything in his soul. His whole life was hanging on it.

For the sky is a single, threatening cloud before the storm's fray.

Around midday the shingle maker rested for a few hours. Then he quickly set off again.

The first grumble fell from the clouds. The wind came. The dust was swirling in gently tearing shrouds. The leaves were becoming restless and beginning to tremble. A frisson was running feverishly across gentle waters. Fires were being extinguished in the houses. People were talking timidly. The day quickly shut its eye and fled into the distance. The shadows of evening came trembling.

The shingle maker strode up the Eschberg.

His heart throbbed and the first large drops were pounding on the fearful-sounding wooden rooves.

He hurried.

"But if it isn't, but if it isn't", the thought trembled through him with the fear of what would then have to happen.

"Ah no! — Ah no!"

But his legs were turning to lead the nearer he got to the house.

It was as though his feet were falling into sinking ground. He had to make firm steps to not fall down. Now his steps were thundering up to the illuminated window.

Josepha and Ullrich were sitting at the table.

The rattling startled them. But their door remained locked.

Franz now stood quietly in the dim hallway and breathed heavily and hesitantly a few times.

Then he stepped into his room with cold numbness.

Musty air as always!! —

He wanted to light a match. Only his hands were upset so that the box fell to the floor. Groaning he bent down and grasped around with stiff, weakening fingers. When he felt it, he was no longer able to close his hand.

Finally — finally the light sputtered ...

— The storm began thundering. —

Everything was as he had left it: the bed rumpled, stiff with filth; the cobwebs hanging like heavy dust bags in the corners; the floor black as a stable's floor; his tattered, stinking laundry under the table.

He looked avidly at everything. With hungry eyes, he sucked it all in. Again and again, he began from scratch to contemplate the neglect.

He relished it like an intoxicating poison. It was flaring in him: hot, stifling.

The storm was growing outside. The forest was crying out. The first lightning! and then a thunderclap that shook the house. It was a jolt in the old man's chest. A shrill call of command.

The shingle maker blanched even more and hesitated for a while. But now a terrible storm was beginning: the scourge of rain with its millions of whipping cords pelted incessantly over the backs of the storm clouds so that, howling ferociously, they hunted through the air and blasted lightning bolts from their thirsting throats. The rocks were groaning with sharp-sided throats, the water was laughing in whining delirium.

This exultation of destruction tore away the flickering numbness from the old man's laced up chest and built his fury up into a madness.

"Ha, ha!"

It thrust him out through the door.

He was laughing shrilly the way a derailing train whistles.

Next to the door in the hallway leaned an iron hammer like stonemasons use for stone splitting. He seized it. And when his arm swung the heavy hammer playfully in the air, the full awareness of his ungovernable strength came over him like a wild frenzy.

"Ha, ha!" he screamed over the thunder which rang like iron rods, "Bump! — Crash! — Swish! — Swish!

Better! more, more! — — I'm destroying everything, scream it, everything, everything! — Help me, help me! You must be made poor!"

He spread his arms to the outraged heavens in supplication. In wild dancing steps, he then stormed across the hall. His host's door was still locked.

"Open!" he screamed and kicked at the door.

"Old man, stay out, I advise you!" Ullrich threatened with cracked voice from within and cleared his throat twice.

But two strikes with the hammer and the door fell in pieces into the room.

"Now out!"

With a battle-ready, fired-up oath, Josepha jumped up from the bench. The midget sprung at the invading shingle maker with a knife. The latter caught him by the chest, rammed him against the wall a few times so that he emitted slurring gurgling sounds, and then threw him outside with a mighty swing for the lightning to feed on. The chastised man fell whimpering in the deep puddles.

Horrified, the woman sank over the table, kissing the wood in mad fear.

Meanwhile Franz had pulled the midget from his daze again outside and was now driving him into the distance with threatening oaths. For all the gentleness seemed to have disappeared from the grey-headed old man. In flapping strides, he sprang after the fleeing man. His soul was foaming in furious rattling thoughts, every bone, every fibre of his life was rioting. He dug up earth and threw it gnashing. He groaned. But no scream was as raw and loud, no oath as furious, no gesture as raging as to encompass the entire thirst of his inner being. He would have liked to have thrown himself to the ground and have bitten himself howling.

Suddenly he remembered that the house still stood and was startled. He ran back flying.

When Josepha heard the rumbling steps of the shingle maker, she leapt up. She began to shake, ran around, snatched at everything and let everything fall again. Finally she pulled together her man's tall boots and ran, emitting agitated whinnying noises, past the snorting man into the open air.

"Out! — it's high time. If you dare to return, I'll throttle you like a rabbit!" he roared after her.

Now he began to lay waste to everything. He smashed the windows out and destroyed all the utensils. He took the clothes from the chests and tore them to shreds. With that a gold-filled stocking fell to the floor. When he saw the gold, he went mad. Spitting, he stomped on it again and again so that the stitches burst and the coins rolled around on the floor.

"Cursed money!" he cried and shoved his right heel again and again into the riches, "thrice over, cursed money! You're oppressors, sparkling dogs! Greedy animals that fill themselves up on human blood."

And he stooped down and threw it all out.

Then he threw himself into his work of destruction again. The restless thunder was drumming him into a new storm and the lightning was flashing like flaring torches. He was lashing out around himself in fury. His face was contorted. From time to time, he laughed in raw triumph.

Now everything was destroyed. — Proud and silent, he looked for a while at his terrible work.

Suddenly!

"The roof! The roof!" he cheered and stormed to the loft.

The hammer swished against the shingles so that entire clusters flew into the open air. The storm wedged itself through the gaps. The roof timbers groaned.

"Open up! — Open up!" the shingle maker egged the storm on impatiently. But the quivering beams were still resisting. Then the old man smashed out the boards of the gable wall.

He was not human anymore, he had become part of the blind force of nature. —

Now the roof timbers began to teeter.

"Away! — away! — fall over, dammit! fall over!" he cried enthusiastically and brought himself down to safety. Finally it gave an earsplitting crack and then the wind fled jeering with the roof and threw it clattering onto a nearby stony ridge. The stones of the collapsing chimney fell crashing on the wooden floor. The flood of rain ran rippling down the stairs and the water was soon dripping through all the cracks in the ceiling.

"Haha!"

The shingle maker skipped around amidst the rubble, clapping his hands and laughing joyfully.

"You must be made poor. What I've given, I can also take away again. Haha!"

But the crops were still standing, a beautiful abundance.

Whistling, he seized the scythe and took to the work.

What the storm and rain had not destroyed, he mowed down. The scythe flashed in the light of the distant lightning. His hair hung in streams mazily over his face. His clothes were fouled, in shreds. Bleeding from the many wounds where he had torn himself on nails and splinters, he kept working restlessly.

The whimpering of the exiles was drifting into the distance.

***

Then the rain was falling gentler. The lightning raised its pale head with weary shrugs a few more times. The sky was clearing and the forest breathed in relief. At last it was completely calm like in the heart of a sleeping child, and nothing was heard but the swishing of the restless scythe.

The shingle maker was slowly advancing step-by-step.

The intoxication had left him and when he straightened up, he wiped his hand heavily over his wrinkled brow to wipe away something agonising.

***

The morning eventually came. You could see how the soles of its glowing feet were touching the forest.

Then the last green stalk sank under the annihilating blade of old Franz.

He threw the scythe down and walked back to the house.

While he was walking in, the slight remorse receded completely and a deep laughter came over him.

He felt strong, recovered from the wounds of his humiliation.

The burden of his tormenting dullness and degradation had been washed away.

The pale expanse lay sweeter, more alluring in the depths of his consciousness.

With homesick, ardently outstretched arms, his soul's longing strode towards that flickering intangible.

Its gait was free and floating like the flight of the butterfly, for his being had destroyed the casing of the failed life which had held it captive.

With the reclaimed smile of his restfully blissful childlike nature, he strode through death's door.

In the corner where his wife had died, a long nail was sticking out. He noosed a cord on it.

"Wife, here I come!" he whispered full of timid joy and placed his head in the noose. —

Then the sun came and pressed his eyes shut. — —

Straightened

Now it had happened. His second face had revealed it to him. That is what he called his distrust. Everything had happened as he had said, "She will be gone one day like when you blow out a candle. Whoever the devil seizes by the collar, also ends up having his neck twisted."

Now it had happened.

She had fallen down the stairs, in the middle of laughing, with sparkling eyes to her death. And he — he — had been standing next to her, that cursed cuckoo, and had seen her fall, had frozen in shock as she lay below and a stream of blood poured from her mouth. Then he was wanting to lift her up. He was bending down and tears were falling from his dimwitted, aquamarine eyes. — He — touching — her?! Before — his – eyes!! "Away, you rascal, nobody touches the dying, even if they're alive ..." With that he threw the scoundrel against the wall.

The crybaby did not defend himself, went stumbling down the stairs and staggered outside into the people passing by. He had done that, he, the master rope maker Karl Stark, to his assistant.

Ha, ha — it should have happened a long time ago! Taking action! and not biting his teeth into his own flesh, yes! —

And as he bent over his wife, now lying on the bed in the sitting room, he had to smile contentedly. No, he had not done it around her. That he had owed to himself and his honour. She, even if she was still as beautiful — a pale girl's face with the wrinkles of a fifty year old around her eyes and over her cheeks, the soft, shiny black hair, the forehead like a blank white sheet, the small, red mouth which he had so endlessly liked and so endlessly hated, and especially the eyes! So, they were glowing just so as the long eyelashes slowly rose when the stupid boy went to her and said some nonsense. But she had always looked at him resentfully blinking, as though to say, "Old grey-head, fool!"

But a good man has a good spirit. The women who do not grow old are only hell's stool pigeons. Should it be good christian living which skips in the fifty year old woman like fresh spring water? — Honest beauty gets old! But it leaves everything a pack of lies. This and yet much more besides, his "second face" had revealed to him. If it could only have informed him of the blood which now and then flowed from her mouth gurgling, over her chin, over her white breast.

If the bloody, burning streaks could talk! If he could tear from her heart what resides there, known to no one! Then he would know every-thing exactly! Then he could — yes, what could he? — Nothing! — He shook his right fist downward and pondered. — Yes — actually he was avenged, but every sheep felt that with the horn, that was the punishment. The punishment! — He could not of course have managed such a thing, the d..., as it worked out with her! Her limp hands were shaking with every beat of her heart. Her lips were twitching in pain. Some-times her face blazed in dark fervour, other times the frost of her fever bunched millions of little heaps on her wilted skin. Life struggled in every fibre for possession; in every fibre, destruction sat and fought with it.

But the heart of the man who stood by her bed and saw everything had no emotion, no charity. He was reading the flaming letters of jealousy again like thirty years before.

It made him hard as stones — — —.

Hasty steps came from the hallway, through the antechamber, to the door. Knocking quickly, the doctor entered.

After a noiseless and quick greeting, the doctor began with fluttering voice, "I heard from the servant woman how it happened. Is it right, Master, the stairs were steep, had fifteen steps and no handrail. Your wife lost her balance with the heavy laundry basket and plunged straight to the ground. Is that right, it happened like that? I have to know so that I have a cause." Stark was about to raise his shoulders to express his disagreement, but he hastily let them fall and quickly stammered, "Yes, yes", and then looked the doctor in the eye searchingly. At the same time, he was thinking angrily, "I'm an old ass who'll yet betray his crime himself. Did he notice anything?"

But the rope maker's anxiety was quite futile, as the doctor had not waited for an answer at all but had immediately begun the examination. After a short period, he turned around and said with a serious face, "Prepare yourself. Your wife has incurred serious internal injuries. Who knows if she'll manage to get through the night. All that I can prescribe are icepacks on her upper body. She will have a high temperature; if she hasn't improved eight hours from now, then fetch me immediately." He gave the master his hand and walked into the antechamber in his company.

But then Stark stopped with a jerk and grasped the doctor firmly on the arm.

"Will she talk madly?" he asked.

"Certainly."

"Do just crazy things come out? Or do those with fever also talk about their lives?"

"Oh yes, of course!"

"Even secrets that no one knows?"

"But why then, master? Yes. But it isn't the same with everyone."

"I mean, can it happen?"

"Certainly it can happen. Many a murder has already come to light that way. The person can only talk about their life!"

"Hm, hm. — I was merely asking, doctor."

The doctor looked at him questioningly, gave a short whistle as a sign that the matter was not clear to him, and left.

Stark stood rooted to the spot, stuck his hands in his trouser pockets and gazed at the floor in front of him for a long time. Then he nodded slowly and a desperate smile which looked like schadenfreude distorted his face.

"Now it comes, now it comes ... everything ... everything. — Now I have to strangle her on her deathbed." And he drew a deep breath in horror. He would probably have stood their pondering for a long time, but the servant woman entered and the patient's groaning came from the room. Stark turned to the old woman who was watching him compassionately because he was bowed as though under the burden of a great sorrow. "Here," he said, "fetch some ice. Get some sheets out and bring it all into the room. Then you can go home."

"But you can't stay alone with the patient! You don't know ..."

"Then you can go home", he cut off her sentence. "I'll do everything myself. I want to be alone with her."

"Now for my sake," the old woman countered astonished and offended, "I'm not a child either, and if, and ..."

"Then you can go home", Stark repeated for the third time with a sharpness that was not at all necessary and he strode to the door.

Everything was soon brought.

The sheets were lying on the commode, the ice bucket was standing next to the chair by the bed, the door was bolted, the servant woman had left. Had she? Women are children. — Stark tiptoed carefully to the door, pulled the bolt back soundlessly and looked inquiringly into the antechamber.

Through the thirty years during which he had been married to his wife and had always had to keep watch over her faithfulness like a flame, he had acquired a great skill in it. Behind the oven, nobody; behind the towels hanging there oddly exaggerated, nobody; under the kitchen table, five iron and three clay pots, and in the largest as always on its soft bed, the black cat, his favourite. The cabinet locked; in the pot cupboard, nobody ... Stark bolted the door to the antechamber as well. Then he returned to the room with long determined steps.

The patient had become restless meanwhile and had shoved the covers half away. Her chest was rising and falling abnormally fast, her lips were moving, trembling. At short intervals she was opening her eyes, looking rigidly at the ceiling and then closing them quickly and fearfully.

Stark folded a sheet and began crushing the ice. Then he paused and pondered.

"No," he said to himself, "no. Afterwards, afterwards. Now she'll talk."

He laid the ice in the bucket again and looked tensely at the patient. Drops of sweat were beading on her forehead, her breath was groaning.

As he watched her wavering in the adversity of death, she who once filled his life with sunshine, a long forgotten feeling of charity came over him from those good tranquil days and seized his heart like the sound of the distant bells in the evening seizes a lost man in the forest.

So he took up the aborted work again and had finished it in a little while.

The patient's temperature was rising. She was tossing and turning in bed groaning, raising herself and weakly falling back again. Stark laid the ice on the disfiguring bloodshot blotches on her still beautiful body — how beautiful! A bitter, acrid fire was clutching his emotions. He repressed it roughly and looked fixedly with glaring eyes into her face, over which a light chill was now running again. From every feature, he read again the long, horrid story of his married life which had brought him his "second face".

But she then opened her eyes and looked at him unsparingly for a long time, gazing fixedly, struggling to clear her vision. Then she stretched her hands out in repulse and sought to shove him away from her in mad violence. Her gaze was helpless, full of terror. "Is it you?" finally ejected from her dry lips fearfully. "You? — Go away — I know you — you are my tormenter ... Your eyes prick like needles ... You are pricking my heart ... it's bleeding ... it's bleeding ... The years are balls of lead ... They are falling on my chest and destroying it ... They are falling on my brain and numbing me ... singing ... singing ... singing!" ... Full of pain in her yearning, her torment, she cries out.

And then she began again, but with a soft, caressing voice, "Oh yes, yes right. Mother! — hold me close and kiss me ... and kiss me ... I'm craving love so much ... for goodness ... for happiness ... Karl! ... Karl!! ... Where are you? ... Don't you see, your life is a pit, and the barren earth is falling over you and burying you ... Why are you cursing? — Curses won't give your soul wings ... Are you fond of the sun, springtime, birdsong ... Your wife? — — — Oh, if could rescue you! — Every man hungers for something. But you — who tells you that you have to consume your heart? No, gnawing ... Let it be — let — people are frivolous — men stupid ... But I have a white dress, pristine like my little communion dress was! ... Why are you hungry for your heart? ... But the day ... the sun ... the sun! ... Where have you gone? — — —

... It's turning to evening — — — and it's all over ... fling the windows open, fling the doors open!! — I must go! — Karl! — — — Look me in the eyes fondly once more, for that is what I hunger for ... Look at — me ... no, not yet! not — yet! ... But the wall is coming ... and flight is seizing me ... Now I'm already far away, over the fields, the mountains ... and a dream is coming to me and leading me — So let's go, you are my angel — you know me ... Do you know him too, my man? ... Don't scowl ... You must have liked him too ... Oh believe me, he can't help himself, he is so fond of me ... but so angry ... Bless, bless him too ... Oh ... I kiss the hand which he stretches out. — — — And now ... it's the whiff of the earth which is strolling towards the sun ... A broad, golden star ... A little ship swinging to it from the flowers which never fade ... we want to sit in it ... Take the rudder, my angel!

And we want to sing too:

> Pretty are the flowers, prettier are men
> in the freshness of youth.
> But they perish,
> have to spoil,

Jesus lives for evermore."

With enraptured, soft voice, she sang herself into death.

The listening air which filled the room was trembling with the lust that it was drinking from the singing soul of the chaste woman. And the soft song filled the room more and more. Then it gradually fluttered away — little by little towards the ceiling like a butterfly floating on soundless wings into the blue sky. Karl Stark stood next to the bed of the moribund, a straightened man, stiff as a statue.

He had pressed his hands over his face. His entire body was shaking. With the cry, "The face, the face!" he collapsed in a faint.

The Visit

If someone could see the reel over which the threads of the days and years of human life were spun!

This ruminating on hopeless desire governed the last ten, fifteen years of Baroness Maria von Borowska's existence. And always, when she pondered these words of mysterious desire or spoke them softly to herself without moving her lips, she felt so close to the secret, like someone listening through a thin wall to the heartbeat of a stranger she cannot reach.

Returning from a walk in the forest on an early spring day, as the young, happy wife of the then first lieutenant Fritz von Borowska, she had surprised her husband in the little forest hut in the arms of the governess. It struck her like a fatal thrust of a sword. Something died in her with the weak cry with which a songbird falls dead out of the air. Without a sound, she stepped back from the window through which she had seen the infidelity of her husband, and returned to the castle. She watched the lustrous spring clouds breaking up in the blue sky as if they were blown asunder. There was a cracking as if the young branches were being broken all over the world. She did not cry out, did not accuse her husband, but went home, had her bags packed, went to the bed of her little son, kissed the sleeping child once, twice softly, timidly on the mouth and departed the same night without saying goodbye.

On the journey south, her ruminating over the meaning of life began. Not only had her marriage of seven years been trodden down, fouled, degraded, but also all the dreams of her childhood, all the maidenly addictions and delights which had lead to them. "Never again back to Germany! never again." That was the only thought on her escape in the express train. And when the thundering of the depths began in the Gotthard tunnel and the wagon was shaking as if being hit by iron rods on the top and sides, she shut her eyes and prayed fervently for the rocks above to collapse onto the train, crushing and burying it.

But two days later she was travelling on a small Italian steamer from Locarno to Pallanza, on Lake Maggiore. The customs officer stopped by her and checked her luggage. He dealt with this business with the most select suavity, with many apologies, merely cursorily, and now and then he lightly touched in homage the genteel, beautiful lady with the pale, helpless face and the shaking hands. So many discreet commiserations, so many enthusiastic devotions spoke from the fire of his large, dark eyes that she lost control of her anguish and asked him if he knew about the reel on which the threads of the days and years of human life are spun. Those standing around stared at her as though she was crazy, the young Italian made a frightened face and bowed self-consciously. She sank into her seat with closed eyes and then stared with a rigid, dry eyes across the smooth lake. But she did not tremble anymore, except for her upper lip. Towards evening the ship went past the ruins of the moorish castle almost sunken under the water. The view of these ruins, dedicated to a slow, though certain decline, calmed her.

Marie von Borowska remained true to her resolution. She sent her husband's letters back unopened, never asked after her son and also behaved dismissively towards all her father's attempts at reconciliation. He finally stopped wanting to discourage his unhappy, lost daughter from her almost inhuman obstinacy and limited himself to providing her richly with financial means, because she passionately refused to accept a single penny from her husband, whom she, however, did not want to divorce but let know that the reunion would certainly only take place when all the ice had melted away from her heart.

So, buried and alive, dead and breathing, she lived under her maiden name of Baroness von

Trüppelt on the shores of the long lake, always in sight of Isola Bella, though she never set foot on it, in winter in Pallanza, in the hot season on the facing cool shore in Stresa. Her father died, she did not hurry to his grave. Her mother followed her deceased husband, she remained in her voluntary exile. Her husband became a Corps Commander. Her son, Dagobert, entered the Military Academy, became a lieutenant in the Dragoons. It all left her unmoved.

She watched the flowers bloom, the butterflies colourfully fluttering about, people laughing and being sad, the lake glittering and darkening. Towns were reflected in the lake. Villages lay dreamily in the valleys. Stars twinkled and paled, seasons came and went. She sank emotionlessly, insensibly into the whirl of existence, and her heart only ever asked the one thing, "Why? Why everything? Why me? Why everyone?"

In this helpless astonishment, in this abysmal sinking, she was living, was not hollowed out, not calcified, not destroyed. The state of being forgotten just deepened in her without pain, without happiness, without bitterness, without mirth. Only her upper lip became shorter from the inner tremor that she could not control, and her eyes lost their lustre. Pale and beautiful like a sleep-walker, she wandered restlessly. As the ghostly moon stands over the forest in the bright sky of day, a pale memory of the night, so she stood in life.

The Great War drove her out of Italy. Her fatherland remained barred from her heart, which had loved too purely, too boundlessly, and, disappointed, no longer found its way back to life.

In Lucerne, where she had taken up residence, she received after many redirections the news of her husband's death in the storming of Liege, and a few weeks later her son fell in the Battle of the Marne.

That tore the iron clasps from her being. The first tears entered her eyes and streamed soundlessly, heavily down her face. She did not wipe them away but let them flow. She sat day and night without sustenance and did not stir from the chair in which she had sunk.

Finally she raised herself and travelled back to Germany, still stunned by the silence of the grave in which she had spent fifteen years, but at the same time calmed in an incomprehensible way, as if satisfaction had been finally given to her for a mortal wrong. And a vague hope was creeping into her heart, which like a dark, ambiguous intimation had never left her. Now she was with both the dead far away from the earth on the other side, so to speak, and greeting them consolingly from there. But what she should hope for, she did not know. Yet, under the urging of this mild, merciful certainty, the long-lasting, deep-lasting sand belt of her reclusive banishment was melting, and while she was being driven through the various parts of Germany by the rigours, by the ghastly unrest and human poverty of the pitiless, almost endless world war, her entire former life, seemingly sunken for ever, was rising in her so forcefully, so tangibly, so concretely and becoming her own again as if her hours and days only took place in it. The capitulation of Germany in November 1918 completed this puzzling transformation which appeared, and had to appear, to everyone as a madness.

She was now styling herself Her Excellency von Borowska again and had established herself with the sumptuous furniture from her husband's residence — he had long since sold the castle and estates — in a five room residence in the small Silesian spa town of Warmbrunn, took into service a companion, a cook and a parlour maid, and began living in style like before her catastrophe and continued this absurd luxury for a period despite the high prices and inflation, until finally she had used up most of her fortune and had actually become solely reliant on a not overly large annuity and the widow's pension. She was compelled to discharge all the servants but for a girl, but preserved under the most severe deprivation the appearance of a noble existence.

She subsisted only on vegetables, dry bread and black, unsweetened coffee from barley corns. But the table had to be decked in white and overloaded with precious porcelain and silver plate like a noble, great dinner table. Fat, butter, cheese and sausages were never absent from the supper table, even if they were never disturbed, but, spread out again and again, having long since spoiled and dried out.

At the principal meals, she appeared in formal dress and walked beforehand through the flight of rooms to see whether anything had been forgotten for the great reception, calling to the only maid sometimes as a support, sometimes as a companion, as cook, servant or coachman and giving her the various assignments: not to let the poulards get too brown, to help the company with their coats, to pick up the counts from the train, to place the sheet music on the piano, to put the wine on ice. At the same time, she ran from window to window and looked out full of expectation to see if guests were calling in.

Then the girl has to open the door and call loudly that it is served. Her Excellency von Borowska appears from the back room and converses with a twittering voice animatedly to the left and right as though she is surrounded by a numerous, illustrious company. Patronisingly she bows sometimes to one side, sometimes to the other as though emblazoned guests were thronging around her to catch some of the shimmer and the charming amiability of her blond beauty.

After the meal, she holds court, converses for a while with ever softer voice and then falls asleep exhausted in her fauteuil. Usually she starts skittishly from the room, looks back into the room disappointed and then asks the deep, noiseless calm with sorrowful voice,

"Is my husband still not here and Dagobert, my son, also not?"

But there is no answer. In the drawing-room, the clock strikes the hour with a deep, singing voice. Then it is quiet again like over the windless mirror of the sleeping Lake Maggiore.

Her Excellency von Borowska sits sorrowfully with tense fingers in her lap and looks with wide, dazed eyes at nothing for a long time until she hears something which falls through the air like the breathless, shrill cry of a dying bird, or until it sounds like the piercing melody with which a precious glass smashes, or until it whistles softly as though a sharp sword is ripping through the air.

Then she shivers, rises painfully and creeps into the small back room which she closes up and bolts shut. After a while she begins to sob louder and louder, more and more heartrendingly and asks without break, "Why don't you come to me? Fritz, Dagobert, come at last!"

On a Sunday in spring 1921, her desire finally materialised. Already in the night that preceded this day, she had experienced something strange.

She awoke after hours of dreamless, refreshing sleep because she had been called by a familiar voice. Just as she had completely shaken off her sleep, the voice's echo resounded around her, but she could not recognise it, even though she knew that she had heard it once before, even that the person who it stemmed from had once been very familiar to her. And while she chased the echo with her ear in wistful desire, it retreated further and further into the distance, became duller, vaguer and in the end was pulsing in weak, rhythmic beats as though it was a heart from outer space, and just then, as she anxiously wanted to take hold of the idea that it was the heartbeat of a late beloved person, she sensed that she had been fooled by the sound of her own heart.

The next morning she arose fresher than usual, primly happy, rejuvenated. The madness of her previous life had been wiped away as if it had never gained power over her. The maid was neither companion, nor support, nor coachman or servant, but just "dear Anna". The grand phoney meals ceased, the courtly attire did not leave the wardrobe, and after her afternoon coffee, Her Excellency von Borowska let the maid go out, although she had not asked.

Once the girl was out of the house, the general's wife struck out for her own walk. It was a beguilingly beautiful, wantonly sunny spring day. The sky was cloudless in delicate, just as bashful blues. The buds of almost every tree were bursting. The lawns and winter grains were a blissful green. The Riesengebirge was like a soundless, grandiose festive music in the heights, its snow covered peaks the only white clouds in the sky. The larks were shooting up into the air everywhere like singing rockets, and the forests were coloured an even dreamier blue than usual by the blissful singing. On the edges of the fields, the blooming blackthorn hedges were dancing like white-clothed maidens.

The general's wife had been lifted by the night's experience from the witches' sabbath of her madness into a fresh, healthy awareness of life. Through the magic and delights of early spring, she fell directly into a girlish indulgence, soon left the main road completely and began aimlessly wandering through the meadows, sitting by the blue ponds to observe the mirage of the reflected mountains, straying among small bushes, plucking anemones and then throwing them away laughing like a child, and when the evening bells chimed, she caught herself humming along to them as they went out from their towers across the fields. From the last blackthorn bush that she encountered, she broke off a handful of sprays.

It was already twilight when she entered her residence, laid the sprays on the table, pushed an armchair to the window and looked outside. The snow covered mountains were smouldering in a light reddish shimmer and, when she had let her eyes rest on them for a while, they became Bürgenstock and Mount Pilatus by Lake Lucerne, then the Monte Mattarone by Pallanza. She was not sitting in her armchair in Warmbrunn, but on the shore of Lake Maggiore. Her father's estate emerged from her memory, the castle with the park of her husband, the meadow behind it, the forest. She was carried through her whole life without any sense of time or space. And at the last, the little forest hut stood before her inner eye, the hut in which her husband's criminal love had uprooted her life.

Her heart was throbbing, a light feeling of powerlessness was enveloping her in a fog, and the mysterious expectation was suddenly in her again, the one which had been haunting her for two years, often to the edge of insanity. She still had the strength to walk to the table and grasp one of the blackthorn sprays.

Then it was to her as though there was a knocking down below at the front door. But it sounded so weak, so far away, like she had heard her heartbeat softly penetrating from outer space the previous night, after she had awoken.

It was calling me, the general's wife thought, and now they are coming. And the front door was really opened and youthful, feathery steps were coming up the stairs, stepping without ringing into the antechamber and covering the way to her door on the runner almost soundlessly.

The general's wife clutched the blackthorn spray with both hands like a talisman and inclined her head abjectly.

When she dared to raise it, her son Dagobert was standing in the blue uniform of a Dragoon a step inside her room, already in the darkness of evening, but still clearly recognisable, bolt upright, slim, with an open face and looking at her fixedly with his large, dark eyes. —

The heart of the general's wife skipped with joy and anguish. She wanted to ask if the apparition was really her son or not, but remembered that you must not address spirits, and bit the blackthorn spray in order to say nothing. Then the apparition floated towards her, clasped her and raised her up.

With a joyful cry, she let herself be carried away.

When the girl barged in, the general's wife was lying lifeless next to the table and had a blackthorn flower in her clenched, discoloured mouth.

A solitary drop of blood hung on her chin.

About the Publisher

Our mission is to provide translations into English of the complete works of neglected major European writers. We do not cherry-pick works that seem the most marketable, but rather seek to provide a complete collection of each writer's works so that readers can follow the writer's development and decide on its merits for themselves.

Printed in Australia
AUOC010802140612
252660AU00001B/8/P